Dana Grigorcea is a Sw... was born in Bucharest i... German-speaking world ... in German. She has been  ...worldwide for her novels and short stories, which have been translated into ten languages. She was awarded the 2011 Swiss Literature Pearl for her debut novel *Baba Rada*, and the German 3sat Prize 2015 for *An Instinctive Feeling of Innocence*, which was also shortlisted for the Swiss Book Prize and the Literature Prize of the German Business Association. In 2020 the French edition of her novel *The Lady with the Maghrebi Dog* was nominated for the Madame Figaro Award. In 2023 Grigorcea received the Romanian Order of Cultural Merits. *Dracula Park* was longlisted for the 2021 German Book Prize and awarded the Swiss Literature Prize. Grigorcea also writes for children.

Imogen Taylor was born in London in 1978 and has lived in Berlin since 2001. She is the translator of Sascha Arango, Dirk Kurbjuweit and Melanie Raabe, among others. Her translation of Sasha Marianna Salzmann's *Beside Myself* was shortlisted for the 2021 Helen & Kurt Wolff Translator's Prize and the Schlegel-Tieck Prize 2020.

DRACULA PARK

Dana Grigorcea

Translated
by
Imogen Taylor

SANDSTONE PRESS

First published in Great Britain in 2023 by
Sandstone Press Ltd
PO Box 41
Muir of Ord
IV6 7YX
Scotland

www.sandstonepress.com

First published in German under the original title: Die nicht sterben, by
Dana Grigorcea © 2021 by Penguin Verlag, a division of Penguin
Random House Verlagsgruppe GmbH, München, Germany

ISBN: 978-1-914518-21-8
ISBNe: 978-1-914518-22-5

Sandstone Press is committed to a sustainable future.
This book is made from Forest Stewardship Council ® certified paper.

MIX
Paper | Supporting
responsible forestry
FSC® C171272

Cover design by kid-ethic
Typeset by Iolaire, Newtonmore
Printed and bound by CPI Group (UK) Ltd, Croydon, CR0 4YY

When they become such, there comes with the change the curse of immortality; they cannot die, but must go on age after age adding new victims and multiplying the evils of the world; for all that die from the preying of the Un-Dead become themselves Un-Dead, and prey on their kind. And so the circle goes on ever widening, like as the ripples from a stone thrown in the water.

BRAM STOKER, *Dracula*

For Perikles

Contents

I

Johnny and His Death

I HAVE NO CHOICE BUT to tell this story, especially as I witnessed everything at first hand and know all reports to be false. The reasons for this – overhasty research, journalistic incompetence, sensation-mongering and, of course, private interests – are not something I shall dwell on; the very thought of them plunges me into a resigned stupor that would be detrimental to my narrative. As for the place where everything happened, I shall simply call it B., partly because I have no desire to add to its notoriety, and partly because the story is emblematic of Wallachian morals in general – though it could, to be sure, have happened anywhere in the world.

By way of orientation for those of you not familiar with the affair, I should mention that B. is a small place in Wallachia, south of Transylvania, at the foot of the Carpathian Mountains. The people from Bucharest and Brașov who had second homes here referred to it simply as a village, while the locals spoke defiantly of a town, because of the big weaving mill that had once stood on the river and made workers of a great many peasants. For my family, ever conciliatory, B. was a charming health resort. On one thing, however, everyone was agreed: until the events of which I shall relate, B. was associated neither with Dracula nor with any other vampire stories.

Before the political turnaround in 1989, you could rent entire villas for the holidays here in B. and we always chose the same one, on the edge of the forest. Villa Diana, named after the famous hunting goddess, was a house like a castle, though years of botched additions had left it misshapen. A balcony with a balustrade ran the length of the first floor, but the plain, whitewashed walls gave an overall impression of sobriety. Shadows loomed on these walls when the surrounding trees stirred in the wind, and in the shifting light of sun and moon they folded themselves bizarrely around the corners of the house.

We travelled there from Bucharest with our extended family and friends in a convoy of cars laden with all Great-aunt Margot's goods and chattels: bed linen, cushions, silver candlesticks, the big Persian carpet for the drawing room, hundreds of icons, a large, silver-framed mirror and all kinds of Turkish şabres and Arabian plates to hang on the high walls.

Within a day the villa was cleared of what Margot referred to as 'dreadful communist kitsch'. She took great delight in holding up pieces of macramé for our delectation. 'Just look at this,' she would say, and with one voice we would cry, 'Oh, don't!'

'But look at this little fisherman with a glass fish on a string,' she would insist.

'Oh, don't!' we would say again.

My mother warned us to take care – we wouldn't be allowed back if we broke anything, she would say, packing everything carefully into wooden crates: the rolled-up tapestry with the pictures from *Il Seraglio*, the stuffed squirrel, even the frosted-glass lamps.

'Do you really want to sit in candlelight?'

'Well, we certainly don't want to sit in the light of *those* lamps!'

And she carried everything down to the cellar.

Any furniture that Margot took a dislike to had to be covered in white dust sheets. We would laugh as the things vanished under their covers, pretending that we had magicked them away.

Finally, cheered on by her friends and relations, Margot would tour the house with a soupspoon full of smouldering incense, to smoke out the ghosts of the *basse classerie*, at least for the duration of our stay.

Liberated from its cornucopia of elaborate glass ornaments, the Ibach grand could now be opened. Anyone who could play the piano was allowed to bang out the Radetzky March or a droll bit of the Romanian Rhapsody, while the rest of us clapped and shouted, fired up by the shrill notes of the out-of-tune instrument.

Then we sat around the big table on chairs and stools, leaning against one another in exhaustion, frozen in thought – a picture in chiaroscuro. Thinking back to the scene, I am inevitably reminded of Rembrandt's painting *The Anatomy Lesson of Dr Nicolaes Tulp*: a solemn-looking gathering dressed for the anatomical theatre, all gazing pensively in different directions – only that on our table, instead of a corpse awaiting post-mortem, there was a plate heaped with biscuits, chiefly the sponge fingers I was so fond of. I used to dunk them in red raspberry lemonade, while the shadow of death lurked just out of sight, behind the brass plates on the high walls.

'Have a look around, darling,' Margot would say, deeply moved. 'It's almost like old times.'

'Wonderful!' I said fervently, to please her – or perhaps just to give myself courage, because, out of the corner of my eye, I thought I saw some of the shrouded furniture shift almost insensibly.

What startled me most was the groan of the parquet: a dull creak beneath the carpet and the preposterous absence of that creak when we moved on.

I remember the chill of that house, the musty smell and the heady mixture of incense and ladies' perfumes. I also remember that the candles were always going out – blown out by a draught, or by a mischievously inclined guest. Our guests were comfortingly noisy; they spoke and laughed a great deal, traipsed all over the house, made late-night pots of tea, played cards, and then set off on midnight walks, returning soon afterwards amid riotous laughter and exaggerated cries of, 'Sh! We're making too much noise.'

Then one of them would start to sing, 'Zitti, zitti,' and the others would fall about laughing.

This 'zitti, zitti' came from an anecdote told by one of our guests – Geo, a baritone at Bucharest Opera House. Geo had told us about a performance of *Rigoletto* in which the choir had to carry such a heavy ladder across the stage in the abduction scene that they were out of breath even before they began to sing – and when they tried to intone the quiet aria, 'Zitti, zitti, moviamo a vendetta', the intense effort required to make any sound at all sent the words bursting out of them in a roar: 'Zitti, zitti – softly, softly, we seek our revenge.' This raucous 'softly, softly' was so startling that the audience broke into peals of laughter.

And so it became a favourite game of Margot and the guests – along with blowing out candles – to creep up on each other and sing, 'Softly, softly, we seek our revenge,' at the tops of their voices.

Then, of course, there was the river that ran through the forest behind the villa and was sometimes dyed red because of the nearby mill. When this happened, one or other of the guests could always be relied upon to appear on the balcony and cry with outstretched hand and quivering voice, 'And all the waters that were in the river turned to blood.'

Looking back, I must say we had excellent fun in those days; our guests were fond of a good joke and forever making each other laugh. Laughter seemed to be de rigueur for guests and hosts alike.

A small path led from the courtyard to a tennis court where we often played; in my memory, the sun is always shining on the red sand. I played with local friends of the family and sometimes we were joined by others from B. We practised doubles. Margot, who always wore full whites and dressed me to match, didn't miss a single game. In those days we had wooden tennis racquets, and the top of my black lacquered racquet was stuck with sticking plaster to stop the wood from splintering when the frame touched the ground. I can still hear the satisfying *plop* of the ball on the racquet, the syncopated rhythm of stroke and counterstroke.

All summer and sometimes even in winter, I stayed in B. with Margot. Although a great-aunt, she was no older than my mother, but she had the old-fashioned, queenly manner of my grandmother, her sister from Great-grandfather's first marriage. I sometimes called her Mamargot.

In my head I have an overexposed picture of us, sitting on the garden bench outside the villa: Mamargot is holding her head high, so that the sharp line of her chin clearly separates light from shade. Her white hands encircle my waist and I – perhaps seven at the time, a skinny, almost scrawny thing, squinting and frowning at the sun – am hung with Mamargot's necklaces, rings and earrings.

'You can do what you like when you're with me,' she had told me, adding, as an example of audacity: 'You could even shave off an eyebrow, if you wanted.' Legend has it that I really did shave off my left eyebrow, but I have no recollection of it; I know only the excited rumours reported by our more regular guests: 'Remember the time you shaved off your eyebrow?'

The most daring exploits I recall from that time took place in the gleaming azure-blue telephone box at the garden gate. Whenever I had a coin to hand, I would push it into the slot, grind out a number – any number – on the stiff dial and listen for a few breathless moments to the strange voice asking who was speaking. Then I would hang up without having said a word. At other times, I overcame my shyness and began to talk frantically: had their house also been damaged by water? When were they going to return their library books? Was it their cooking that smelt so delicious? What were they having for lunch? I was always amazed at the willingness of these unsuspecting strangers to let me engage them in conversation.

On one occasion, an elderly lady gave me her own version of the traditional cozonac recipe; she told me she had spent decades perfecting the sweet bun loaf. 'Have you got that?' she kept asking, as she dictated.

'Yes,' I lied.

In all that I tell you, you will see sinister signs, portents of what was to come. You will look for harbingers of the shocking facts, the unimaginable atrocities, the death of all deaths.

Some of you will be inclined to associate the events with Romania's barbaric Communist regime – to see them as a result of the forty-year dictatorship that is said to have bred a new race of humans. You will stress the need to look at things in their historical and geographical context. And I agree with you – albeit from a rather dubious position. After all, I am no different from the rest of my kind and in judging them, you also judge me. To be sure, I had the privileges of class and education; I could, in theory, have done anything with my life. But I stayed; I went abroad only briefly and then I came back. Yes, I sat and watched it all happen, like a rabbit staring at a snake.

It is this experience that I wish to tell you about, candidly and without embellishment, inching my way towards the ghastly truth.

I didn't see it coming – and here, as if in proof of my unconcern, I am reminded of the white chalk marks that I made so dutifully on the tennis court every morning, the mild sunlight on my arms and the heady mountain air in my nose: narrow lines, drawn neatly on the red sand with the one-wheel marking rod, a squeaky affair in green-painted tin.

Afterwards I would draw and paint for hours on end – or my friends Tina and Arina would join me on the balcony and we would make fake nails out of petals: yellow from the coneflowers; pink and white from the cosmos. At other times, we lay on the grass looking up at the sky and watched the clouds clotting into shapes: horses rearing up on their hindlegs, knights with drawn swords, castles with citadels, fluttering pennants, princesses with conical headdresses trailing veils, waterfalls and rushing torrents carrying mighty tree trunks. No other skies, we were sure, contained such a wealth of heroic images. This was partly, of course, the influence of our national communist history lessons which gave a disproportionate amount of time to the heroes of the Middle Ages, but it was also a symptom of our childlike megalomania, our unshakeable belief that we were in the right place and destined for great things.

When I was on my own, I read a great deal, especially the adventure novels of Jules Verne, Alexandre Dumas and Karl May. In between times, I would stroll through B. with Mamargot and her friends, the heroes teeming in my head.

I mention these joyful walks as evidence against myself, because, though I looked about me as attentively as any of my heroes, I noticed nothing. I examined the drooping branches of the spruces that lined the way to our house; I studied the patterns in the rough, friable bark. Yes, I subjected everything to minute scrutiny in those days, sensing that the world was full of mysterious signs – that I had only to study the spruce bark for long enough and great things would be revealed to me: the secret of life, or at least the secret of some immense treasure.

Some way up the hill, just past the first fork in the road where an enormous beech tree had been felled, I gathered bunches of blue and yellow flowers: chicory, scabious and meadow sage; dandelions, kidney vetch and cowslips. Dear Mamargot, who called me an 'artistic soul' even then, teased me for this, but always kept vases ready for me – in winter I filled them with armfuls of spruce. We sometimes looked at a book of Ștefan Luchian's flower paintings together, and Mamargot would tell me the story of his life – how he had begun to suffer from paralysis in 1900 when he was only thirty-one, and how he'd had his paintbrush tied to his hand so that he could go on painting. His illness didn't break him, Mamargot said, just as nothing would break us.

And I would lie in her arms, looking at the pictures of vibrant red poppies, carnations, cornflowers, wild flowers, chrysanthemums, roses, marigolds and Luchian's famous anemones. He sold only one picture during his lifetime – to his teacher – but even failure could not deter him.

One of my favourite paintings was the *Two Muses* with their coronets of flowers – they reminded me of my friends Tina and Arina. Another was the landscape *After Rain*. I approved of Luchian's determination to paint. I also felt there was something right and noble in his years of illness amid all those flowers – and in his early death. But perhaps that was just the way Mamargot told it.

People say that the door to Ştefan Luchian's house was always open, like a church door. The little oil lamps under the icons allowed him to see the shapes of things, even at night. One night, towards the end of his life, when he was hardly able to move at all, a dark figure came to him and produced, from under its long, black cloak, a musical instrument – a fiddle. For the next hours the figure proceeded to fiddle away without a word, and Ştefan Luchian wept because he recognised all the songs.

'Wait,' he is said to have called out, as the figure turned to leave. 'Please tell me who you are.'

The dark figure came back and bent over the dying painter. 'Forgive me for bursting in on you like this. Think of me as a fellow artist who loves you.'

In the light of the little oil lamps, Luchian recognised the composer George Enescu.

'George Enescu!' Mamargot cried with shining eyes. 'It was the great Enescu!'

'Where are the ladies of the house?' Someone was calling us. There was always a good deal of coming and going in Villa Diana: our friends who arrived in a steady stream throughout the summer; holidaymakers from Bucharest and Brașov who rented villas here – and even a fair number of locals, some of them from neighbouring towns and villages. They all came bearing bunches of roses and wild flowers, armfuls of lilac and fir.

'Look how magnificent!' Mamargot called to me from between the hall and the drawing room. 'Where am I going to put them all?'

It was a well-guarded secret in our house that we had someone at the goat farm in the next village, down in the valley. The goats were kept in sheds in what had once been a very grand house belonging to Mamargot's godparents: a long building with white Doric columns, wide windows and an imposing entrance with a flight of marble steps where, once upon a time, the coaches had stopped and Mamargot's godmother had been welcomed by the cook – because, of course, her first concern as lady of the manor was for the day's menu. There were still photographs of this house and Mamargot liked to tell us about it in great detail – and about the surrounding acacia wood where she had ridden as a girl before it was cleared by the Communists.

As I was saying, then, we knew someone who lived in the grand white house that was now a goat farm. We called him Johnny, though I don't think that was his real name. I can't remember – if, indeed, I ever knew – how we were informed of his prospective visits. But I do know that on the days Johnny was due, our friends always began to sing that Edith Piaf song at a very early hour of the morning:

Johnny, tu n'es pas un ange,
Ne crois pas que ça m'dérange...

Everyone would be bustling about excitedly, when suddenly, unexpectedly, someone would sigh and burst into song:

Johnny! Johnny!
Johnny! Johnny!
Si tu étais plus galant,
Johnny! Johnny!
Johnny! Johnny!
Je t'aimerais tout autant.

And they would all laugh, even more uproariously than usual.

Once, when one of our guests asked me what I wanted to be when I grew up, I caused great amusement by saying, 'Johnny's wife.' I must have been about eight or nine at the time.

'Good luck to you!' the guests yelled, laughing. 'Good luck to you!'

'Never,' Mamargot shouted and I remember her anger, because it was rare for her to lose her temper. 'Never will she marry that poor Johnny! Stop this madness, all of you!'

But I continued to sing the chorus of the Johnny song to myself, especially when I played tennis:

(*Moaning*) 'Johnny!' (*a serve*)

'Johnny!' (*a second serve*)

'Johnny!' (*a crosscourt forehand and a dash for the net*)

(*Drawing out the words*) 'Oh, Johnny!' (*a topspin volley*)

One day I would marry Johnny, I was sure of it. And Mamargot would end up admiring me for it, just like all the others.

I began to think more and more about Johnny from the white house; I had a clear picture of him. He was tall and thin with combed-back hair, a long nose and an elegant squint. He raised ladies' hands to his lips and bowed gallantly. I thought of him as I dashed about the tennis court in the early-morning dew; I thought of him when I ran my damp fingers over the sticking plaster on my black racquet or caught a glimpse of a startled bird; I thought of him when my friends weren't around and I had to stick petals on my nails all by myself, as the pump creaked in the garden.

And time and again I was struck by the sense that the world was full of messages to me and that everything was pushing me in one direction, towards a great future – a future with Johnny from the grand white house.

One day I decided that the next time Johnny came to visit, I would try to get a good look at him. This meant staying up late, because Mamargot had said he always came in the middle of the night. I didn't dare ask to be woken when he arrived, and so I waited at the window.

I waited a long time. I remember that the night was dark but filled with stars, the Milky Way a white wisp, just like our garden path of white pebbles gleaming in the moonlight. There was a smell of fir resin and chill night air. The river roared softly in the forest; close by, an owl called.

Outside my open window I saw Johnny in the light of the streetlamp – a figure in a hat and a dark coat, powerfully built, to judge by his silhouette.

Margot went out to meet him. She opened the gate and led him through the garden.

'We've missed you,' she said, almost in a whisper. 'I thought you'd forgotten us.'

I heard her turn the heavy key in the lock, and a moment later I heard Johnny's hoarse, cracking voice on the stairs: 'No, of course not! How could I forget you? Dear Madame! For whom do you take me?'

I crept out of my room. I passed the dark-blue gleam of the open grand piano and a bulky piece of furniture covered in a shimmering white dust sheet. I saw our friends gather around Johnny and push him towards the kitchen. He still had his hat on; it towered over everyone's heads.

'You'd forgotten us, admit it!'

'Dear Madame! Of course not! I just haven't had the chance.'

'Oh, come on, you'd forgotten us.'

'How could I forget you?'

'A glass of water?'

'Let him take his coat off first.'

I walked barefoot towards the kitchen, moving slowly, ever so slowly, over the creaky places in the parquet. Outside the kitchen I felt a stream of colder air.

Someone, a woman, gave a cry of delight, and the others hissed, 'Sh! Not so loud!'

'Zitti, zitti.'

I heard muted laughter.

I remember the light: it grew redder towards the ceiling and seemed to flicker up, casting leaping shadows. Soon I could see the steam from our friends' breath and from their warm bodies – and, peeping into the kitchen, I saw their many arms: sinewy arms, thrashing the air, groping hands that curled to claws and pierced the flesh.

'Faster, faster,' they whispered with one voice, and a thick column of steam rose above them.

Their hands tore feverishly at the flesh.

'This is a lovely piece – look at this!'

'You haven't seen this one!'

'Ah!'

And in the middle of the guests and their flailing arms, I saw Johnny, stark naked and gleaming with blood, his powerful body stripped of its skin.

Chunk after chunk they tore from his body – from his chest, his belly, his legs. They heaped all the pieces onto big plates.

I remained in the doorway, staring at the man who lay there in mute endurance, growing gradually smaller and slighter. Beneath every layer of flesh, a new sheet of cling film was waiting to be ripped off, until our friends had peeled him right down to his pale body, revealing dark, damp hair on his chest and belly.

Before them lay a tall, skinny boy with drooping shoulders, dressed in bloody underpants.

Someone brought him plastic mules so that he could go to the bathroom and have a shower.

'Are you sure you don't want us to heat up some water for you?'

'No, merci, I can't stay long.' Johnny laughed. 'I always have cold showers anyway; it's good for you.'

Despite his thinness, he had a child's chubby face. Was it my imagination, or did he have dimples, too?

'Wonderful fellow!' I heard our friends say. 'You have to admire him!'

The following summer, Johnny, our man from the goat farm, stayed away even longer than usual – and then I heard our friends say that the wolves had got him in the forest one night. I didn't know if they meant real wolves or Securitate agents, and I didn't ask. But I felt sorry for Johnny.

For a while I still thought of him when I played tennis. When the branches stirred in the wind, it seemed to me that he might come out of the forest and watch me play.

No, of course not! How could I forget you?

Sometimes, a sound from the forest reminded me of a long-drawn-out note from an accordion: *Johnny, tu n'es pas un ange . . .*

But as time went on, I more or less stopped thinking about him.

II

The Lecherous Goat

WHEN THE DICTATORSHIP came to an end in 1989 the villa was restored to us. Margot had the engraved sign saying *Villa Diana* replaced by a new one that read *Villa Aurora* in copperplate lettering. The communist kitsch, as she called it, was banished to the cellar to await the appropriate refuse collection, and she did out the house in a rustic style, with Biedermeier furniture, Orthodox icons, her big silver-framed mirror, the Turkish sabres and Arabian plates from her father's travels, and paintings of rural life in Romania. Her exquisite taste was much praised by our friends; she had, they said, done a more stylish job than Queen Maria back in the day in nearby Bran Castle.

Our friends indulged Mamargot in her penchant for compliments, while she, for her part, was never less than generous and always ready, not to say eager, for a bit of ceremony.

'You're looking splendid, Margot!'

'Well, look at you, my dear, you're magnificent! Did you have a good journey?'

'Not great. The roads are ghastly, but this resort of yours is a dream. Arcadia!'

'It's only Arcadia now that you're here!'

'This air! It's like breathing for the first time.'

'Isn't it glorious? And can you hear the birds?'

'What kind are they?'

'Wall creepers.'

'They're enchanting!'

'Aren't they? Let us drink to them in the garden.'

The garden at the front of the house was always a mass of flowers: phlox, hydrangeas, dahlias, and everywhere roses – red roses, yellow roses, heady-scented damask roses. Everything flowered at once – hyssop and thyme, tarragon and St John's wort. Neighbours would come by and call out from the gate, 'I'll just pop this into the earth, then I'll be on my way,' and Margot would blow them a kiss and press them to stay for a glass of wine and a piece of cozonac – a new plant called for celebration and the cozonac was from Capşa in Bucharest and not to be missed!

I never saw Mamargot doing any weeding; sometimes a guest would feel the urge to set to, or a neighbour who had only meant to drop by.

'It all looks so lovely as it is,' Mamargot would say; even the weeds thrilled her when they came into flower – and the milk thistles with their purple heads.

Down by the lilacs at the end of the pebble path was the garden table with its two benches, and beside it the water pump with three wooden buckets where we cooled watermelons and bottles. The pump could often be heard going during the day; its metallic creak became a familiar sound to me, as soothing as the babble of our guests.

'I fall asleep best,' I am said to have remarked as a child, 'when I can *just* hear our guests talking outside.' Friends sometimes recalled this when praising us for our hospitality: clearly I had inherited my great-aunt's natural flair.

'Home is where one is host,' Mamargot would say. She certainly entertained a brisk flow of visitors.

One of these, a rather officious neighbour called Sanda, ended up being elevated to the status of housekeeper. I will admit straight off that Sanda spooked me out. Missing molars had left her with sunken cheeks, which produced unsightly shadows on her face when she joined me for lunch in the midday sun. She was only in her twenties when she came to us, but very severe and convinced that the world was full of evil and deceit from which she must protect us. Mamargot called her 'my trusty one' and 'Miss Sanda', which she adored; I sometimes saw her twitch with joy.

While the pump creaked and the guests talked and laughed in the garden, I would sit on the balcony, in the sun or shade, or on the line that separated them. I see myself there now, drawing with fierce concentration, my pencils growing smaller and smaller until I was left holding only a stump. I drew with my finger skimming the paper, almost touching it – and yet I found it hard to believe that I was the one drawing.

Looking up, I saw everything in pin-sharp focus. To my right the mountains loomed with their grey-veined crags and pale-green slopes, patches of moorland, jagged lines of firs and jutting trees that grew at intervals from the rock face. Down below, in the dense mixed forest, beech leaves rustled occasionally, shimmering like little mirrors.

Our cheerfully overgrown garden and the road that led from our gate up to the hills, where cows and horses grazed, separated the forest from a few grand villas, some awkwardly-shaped plots of land dotted with haystacks, and some small local farms: low-slung buildings with rusty tin roofs, standing in yards full of dogs and cats, chickens, geese, turkeys.

Looking at these things, I felt once again the joy that had filled me all those years ago as I contemplated this happy existence – the conviction that I was looking at a version of eternity, or paradise. For it was in B. that I first fell in love, and I walked about the place in a state of rapture, thrilled by everything I saw.

The world here seemed tightly serried; everything was close and dear to me: the flashes of light glinting through the high fir branches, the familiar road strewn with scorched cowpats, the pale-green picket fences – and, of course, the people themselves, who despite, or perhaps because of, their lack of sophistication, seemed more of a piece with life, more feeling, maybe even more real than anyone else – like in the paintings by Nicolae Grigorescu that Mamargot had taught me to love.

I knew all the young people in B. and they knew me. They showed me how to cut grass with a scythe and let me fetch their cows from the pasture – not that the cows couldn't find their own way back – and I climbed trees with them and jumped in the straw and sometimes went about barefoot, even, on one occasion, in the rain. How free I felt. And when I talked to my local friends, I spoke like them, in short sentences. I started every sentence with 'well' and sometimes talked in a deliberately muddled way.

I could tell you about my romances in B, but my memories of them have been overshadowed by that ghastly business, that shocking, excoriating business with . . .*the Count*.

The Count and all the suffering he brought down on us: agonising death, unimaginable horror, revenge.

To give you an idea of the man we summoned, little knowing what we were doing, I have looked out a copy of the famous portrait of Prince Vlad the Impaler, known to you as Dracula.

Vlad's features have been said to bespeak a cruel nature. But look closely. All I see here is an expression of embarrassment, a look of acute unease. *Prince Vlad the Impaler of the Romanian Country* was painted sometime between 1462 and 1475 during his long sojourn in Visegrád, at the court of Matthias Corvinus, king of Hungary. Strictly speaking, Vlad was a prisoner there, but he was treated like a prince, almost as a friend of the king. He was even given the king's beautiful cousin Ilona Szilágyi as his wife.

And when Ottoman messengers came, the king would seat Prince Vlad on a little chair next to the throne to put the fear of God in them. Bolt upright he sat on his little chair, the Hungarian chroniclers say, and the Mussulman messengers stared at him wide-eyed. In the Ottoman Empire he was known as 'Kazikli Bey' which means 'Prince Stake'.

The painting shows him in his thirties, his long, narrow face and high, almost feminine cheekbones framed by dark curls that tumble over his shoulders. His complexion is pale, his eyes large. Vlad is pensive, turned away from the viewer; the rings under his eyes look as if they've been there a while. Delicately arching brows dip abruptly to an aquiline nose with flaring nostrils, and – clamped ridiculously between nose and thick lower lip – an exotically curved moustache runs across his face from one hollow cheek to the other.

The impression of noble fragility is further enhanced by Prince Stake's sumptuous get-up: a dainty gold collar stands open at his long white throat, and a closely fitting red velvet coat with a broad collar of sable hints at a rather slender physique. Meanwhile, sticking out of a red velvet cap edged with rows of pearls – and continuing the elegant line of the nose – a cocked heron's feather adorns the princely head, affixed at the forehead by a lavish gold star set with a large ruby and crowned with a semi-circle of five plump pearls. The ruby in the gold star matches the red boyar coat with its gold buttons. If you look carefully, you will see that the line of clunky buttons at Prince Vlad's chest slopes away slightly, as if he were breathing in. All this seems to shimmer in candlelight: the silky skin, the soft velvet, the long hair whose stray locks you want to smooth straight, the sleek sable, the gold twist buttons, the lustre of the pearls.

Only the heron's feather – cut off just short of the upper edge of the painting – describes an unrelentingly straight line.

The portrait is by an unknown German artist, and I try to imagine how another artist of the time might have painted Prince Vlad – an Italian Renaissance artist, say, like Antonello da Messina, who was stared at with such intensity by his sitters. In fact, with his nervous fragility and long, thick locks, Prince Vlad would have made a perfect subject for Botticelli – and just imagine the Vlad that Leonardo da Vinci might have given us.

What a pity that he should have been painted by such an undistinguished and conventional artist. On the other hand, one could argue that conventionality and lack of distinction were similarly de rigueur in Prince Vlad's entourage, where obedient loyalty counted for more than courage.

The prince himself, who was born into wars and spent his life planning battles and cultivating alliances, had precious little to do with artists or scholars. Both before and after his imprisonment in Visegrád, the prince of the Romanian Country inhabited a narrow, circumscribed world, in which he came to feel increasingly under siege.

But enough of that. Now I will tell you the story of the ghastly happenings in B. I call on the prince as my witness – my ancestor Prince Vlad the Impaler, whose blood flows in my veins.

I have put off writing my report on Dracula. The reason is that it took me a while to make the connection between the hideous events I was trying to understand and my own familiar little world. You will, I am sure, appreciate my scruples. My present feeling, however, is that the whole affair can scarcely be understood without reliable eyewitness reports such as would allow you and our descendants to recognise, perhaps, a certain complicity on the part of the witnesses themselves. Only a dim premonition would remain, muddled and obtuse as superstition – and so it is that I want to clear up, once and for all, the confusion surrounding the Dracula legend in B.

All through my childhood there was talk of only one Count Dracula in Romania and that was the blood-sucking dictator Nicolae Ceaușescu.

When his cursed regime came to an end, the Romanian people were, in a sense, free; they had a choice, and many felt that it was time to return to the old values. The word *tradition* was on every tongue. As long as this meant European tradition (whatever that might be), people managed to keep their cool, but as soon as talk turned to national lore, they completely lost their heads. Everyone thought themselves in possession of the true, the unadulterated Romanian tradition; they puffed out their chests, however puny, and vaunted themselves its legitimate heirs and chosen guardians.

Even an otherwise sensible city dweller like Margot was not immune to this celebration of national tradition, although it was the celebrating itself that really interested her – that and the wacky rusticity that she put to such good use in entertaining her guests. She began to spend more and more time in B. Here in the country, she said, away from the mad pace of Bucharest and the *basse classerie* of the new political class, you could live the way people used to. Here you could still have a high old time – some good traditional fun.

As long as I was at school, I spent all my holidays in B., and when I look back on those years I am always reminded of that famous quotation, though I can't remember where it's from: 'Time used to be so patient with me.'

While in B., I read *The Big Book of Folk Legends* and drew historically inspired pictures, mostly along the lines of Theodor Aman's *The Battle with Torches*. I was a firm believer in Aman's prophecy – even now, all these years on, I can still quote it verbatim: 'Great art will be historical, created in such a way that everyone will be able to contribute to its impact – an art which, by recalling past glory, will give us strength and faith for the future.' Encouraged by these words, I read and painted – and with the arrogance of youth, I was convinced I would grow up to be an exceptional artist and a great patriot.

Tennis remained a passion for me, and I played long matches with our guests – matches that seemed to go on forever because the better players were always generous enough to let their opponents keep up with them.

It seems to me, though, that I spent the greater part of the holidays with my friends from B. I went to their farms or walked into the hills with them, or we would wander through the forest and down past the weaving mill to the river, throw stones in the water and wade across to the other side – a test of courage because none of my friends could swim. We crossed the river hand in hand so that I could rescue them if they got out of their depth. And when we were hungry we foraged for hazelnuts and berries, or helped ourselves to the low-hanging apples in other people's gardens.

I think Miss Sanda must have known this, because she was always waiting for me when I got back, clicking her tongue to show her opinion of my behaviour – an exceedingly low opinion.

Her severity made her seem older than her years. None of the young people I hung out with had been to school, she told Mamargot – there was no school in B. and they didn't bother going to the next town. They were too lazy to work on the fields; they did nothing all day long; what they really wanted was to live like us. People here were deeply envious of us – we were blind not to notice. We ought, she said, to be very, very careful.

One thing that always gave Miss Sanda immense satisfaction was to report on friends of mine who had left to live in Spain or Italy. 'Another criminal gone,' she would hiss. 'Thank the Lord.' And it was true that with every passing year I found the place emptier – almost deserted. One by one my old friends moved away; one by one they followed each other abroad – first all the young or relatively young people, and then all the kids too.

B. grew quiet; when I went back there in my student vacations I tended to spend most of my time alone on the balcony or in the garden, drawing or reading, especially biographies of driven, lonely artists – 'subtle seismographs of their society,' to adapt a phrase used of Edvard Munch.

At about this time, my mental picture of Miss Sanda began to come into focus, and an actual picture took shape with her as its subject: *Figure in Goat Costume*, my final exam piece and first pen and wash drawing. It was also the first work I sold – in the National Theatre of Bucharest no less, at the big auction.

I could have bought myself a house in B. with the money – there were several places going for a song. But what would I have done with a house? Set up a studio? Hardly. I was happy painting on the balcony of Villa Aurora. I began to regret having sold the picture.

> *Tsa, tsa, tsa, my little dear,*
> *The wolf is coming very near.*

These words were brayed by a chorus of men, as a figure in a goat's costume pranced around our courtyard, rattling a pair of wooden jaws wildly above its head.

> *Tsa, tsa, tsa, my little dear,*
> *The wolf is coming very near.*
> *Tsa, tsa, tsa, my little goat,*
> *Soon you'll be inside his throat.*

The goat stumbled, rattled its wooden jaws at each of the spectators in turn, then staggered and fell to the ground where it thrashed about in its last throes, twitching rhythmically, following the fate described in the song. It died of fear, a pitiful death.

But hardly had it come to rest than it leapt to its feet again and started capering about, a hump-backed nanny goat frolicking on her hindlegs. The chorus continued its raucous song: everyone knew, they told the goat, that she was looking for a billy goat and lusting for sugar – and when she heard their rhyme, she would wake even from the dead.

It was the traditional goat dance for driving away evil spirits. We gave the old men chocolate, nuts and money, the way we used to with the children, and their leader doffed his cap and said, 'That's it then, ladies and gents, no more evil spirits here.' And the little group of old men went on their way with their goat, and there were hardly any inhabited houses left in B. where they could go to perform their goat dance.

At first the young people came back in the holidays to build houses of their own with the money they'd earned abroad – two- or three-storey constructions on their parents' plots.

'The Italians are coming,' the old folks would say in delight, and they would slaughter their turkeys and chickens and geese and whatever else was still around.

'If not for the kids, then who?'

And for two whole weeks they barbecued and drank and sang and yelled for the grandchildren: 'Giovanni, Matteo, Chiara, Francesca … Dinnertime! Mangiare! Comer! Andale!' Some worked on the scaffolding, while others kept an eye on the barbecue. Billows of blue smoke rose above B. and stereos blasted out music.

'Remember this song?' they shouted.

'Oh yes, we've missed this one!'

'How about this dance?'

And the old man would leap to his feet, shouting, 'Come on, old girl, let's show the Italians how to dance!'

And he and his wife would launch into a wild folk dance, jumping and stamping so that the dust flew. Before long, others were joining in; even the men on the scaffolding climbed down, whooping, and they all danced in a circle with the old couple, spinning faster and faster until the whoops came in jerks. Then the son of the family did some of his old acrobatic leaps, and he broke the circle and led everyone out of the farm in a long line, stepping quickly, cheering loudly. They held each other's waists and leaned their heads on each other's shoulders – 'You didn't think we'd forgotten, did you?' – and danced all the way up the road so that the neighbours could join them, further and further, until I lost sight of them.

In the evenings, Margot had her father's old gramophone carried out onto the balcony; she played Enescu's 'Romanian Rhapsodies' and we lay on the ottomans until late into the night and abandoned ourselves to the music, a silver tray beside us with a glass jug of cold mountain water from the pump, and jam made with rose petals from the garden. The music was tempestuous and wistful by turns; we listened, exhilarated, to the whoops and sighs of the beautiful orchestral arrangement – folkloristic miniatures by the wonderful George Enescu.

I ought to use elements from Romanian folklore in my paintings, Mamargot urged me. And I did, though not in the way she meant – and certainly not in the way our friends would have wanted. No glorification for me. I preferred a bit of deconstructive verve – sometimes even a caricatural approach.

Meanwhile B, too, continued to change – rather more than Margot and her entourage were prepared to accept of their beloved rural idyll. The young people only came every other year and didn't stay as long as they used to – and eventually they stopped coming to B. altogether. The buildings they had put up gradually fell into ruin; only the high concrete walls remained, casting cold shadows on their parents' houses.

III

Homecoming – the Fear

AFTER COMPLETING AN MA at the Académie de la Grande Chaumière in Paris, I returned to Margot in B. I travelled by train via Hungary, which had just become a member of the EU, to Romania, which would be admitted three years later.

It wasn't just my longing for my darling great-aunt that took me straight from Paris to B. You may find it hard to believe, but B. was a home to me.

I felt I knew it better than anywhere else. Sometimes I caught myself looking for B. in other places – for the play of shadows on our white house, the glass-clear air with its drifting patches of haze, the yellow cowslips in the grass, the piping of the little wall creepers as they trilled over and over, 'Please roll your Rs, please rrroll your Rrrs . . .', shrill columns of sound hovering above my raised head.

Because yes, I'd always walked tall in B., gazing up at the high spruces along the edge of the road, mesmerised by the almost imperceptible swish of the branches – a movement through time, but a movement that I noticed quite clearly, for here in B. I knew when to look and I looked with a practised eye.

Home I went then, buoyed up by new knowledge and experience. I could already feel inside me all the pictures and ideas that would come to fruition in B., this place that inspired me more than anywhere else in the world.

'B. is your Tahiti,' said Mamargot, who understood.

And it's true that while in Paris I had sent her some pictures I had painted in the style of Gauguin, with dominant colours applied *à plat* – blue and green and everything up close.

In return I had received a whole heap of letters from her, written in pale-blue ink in her forward-sloping hand with big loops and flourishes and waywardly dotted i's: cheerful reports from B. consisting mainly of anecdotes about her guests and thoughts on my paintings, but also the occasional animal story – about the foxes that ate her hibiscus, or the big bear that rolled down the road some evenings.

Mamargot had come out in her car to meet me at the bus station in the next town.

'Welcome back to Tahiti!' she cried, giving me a fierce hug.

She had grown leaner, sinewy, but she stood tall and straight, and I was amazed at how good she looked with her grey hair; it went beautifully with her tanned skin.

'The mountain air,' was all she said. About time I got some sun and fresh air too, she added.

She was wearing the red leather gloves that she wore to drive and launched into telling me about the guests I was about to meet.

The car drove over potholes, rocking like a boat on a choppy sea – how I'd missed the bumps and jolts. Margot cheerfully listed the friends who were staying. I looked across at her and then past her, out of the window at the low grey clouds pierced here and there by the peaks of the Carpathians – that pattern of forest and rock that I knew so well. Sucked in by it all, I stared up at the mountains so as not to have to look at the dismal state of the landscape at ground level: scorched grass, plastic bags billowing in low bushes, long stretches of toppled fencing, houses whose bricks were exposed by crumbled rendering, foundation pits, pools of murky water, and everywhere concrete ruins – two- or three-storey shells with rusty armatures protruding from the concrete, like fingers stiff with cramp.

The place wasn't what it used to be, Mamargot said. Communism had crippled people – robbed them of any sense of beauty or goodness.

'Look about you,' she said. 'This is what you get when people fail to bear their poverty with humility and a sense of decency. They've wilfully embraced this swanky squalor.' Then, cheerful again, she added, 'Great material for an artist.' Others, she said, travelled thousands of miles to find such subject matter; I had it all here in front of me. 'Powerful, emotive pictures, exemplary pictures!'

We laughed.

An old man driving a goose across the road gave us a friendly wave.

We passed a tall sign that said *Welcome to B.* in blue letters, and underneath *Twinned with Bursa, Cetinje, Djerba, Moissy-Cramayel, Ilyichevsk, Ohrid.*

In front of our house Mamargot leaned on the horn like a wedding guest, and her friends came pouring out. I was greeted with great jubilation – inside, Geo strummed the Radetzky March.

We drank champagne and ate the aubergine salad that I was so fond of – fresh aubergine salad on toast with big, floury tomatoes. All the walls, which had once been hung with Turkish sabres and Arabian plates, were now hung with my pictures, in discreet white frames that set them off beautifully. Darling Mamargot! The house smelt of burnt aubergine skin and there were wild flowers in all the vases. Mamargot had even put red candles in the candlesticks, which she would light the evening.

When it began to rain late that afternoon, the rain matched my mood. I went onto the balcony and looked out over the grey landscape, watching dark-grey rivulets coursing down the tree trunks and houses – they made me think of prison bars. Water streamed down the road over the cracked asphalt, making it darker and darker. The old streetlamp outside the house next door was still there, but it was no longer working.

Whenever it had rained after dark in the past – or blown a gale, or snowed fat flakes – I had always seen it in the yellow light of this streetlamp, and it felt as if that past were breaking away from me for good. Back then, the weather had always had a sense of occasion and an appropriate backdrop. Now it rained as if it didn't care.

At the roadside, a black bird sat on the branch of a beech tree, letting the rain run over its folded wings. The rain fell, loud and steady, and strange feelings of guilt rose in me at the thought that I'd been away for so long and no longer looked on the place as fondly as I should.

The next morning, the rain had stopped and the sun was shining; from my bedroom window I saw Miss Sanda cross the tennis court with the drag net to smooth the red sand for me. I watched her walk from left to right and back again, stalwart as ever, and when she was finished I saw her climb onto the high umpire's chair to inspect her work.

'Thank you, Miss Sanda,' I called out to her from the window. 'Thank you.'

I felt suddenly close to her, grateful, perhaps, that she, at least, was still around – living evidence, as it were, of my wonderful childhood and the rather ludicrous troubles we'd had with her.

In all other respects, even now in such glorious sunshine, B. had become alien to me, almost unrecognisable. This was partly to do with the altered dimensions: in most gardens these days the grass grew as tall as a child, making the houses look darker and shrunken. But there were other changes too: rusty buckets were strewn about the yards; forgotten rakes stood propped against garden fences – and some of the fences that had once meant something to me were gone altogether, as was the wooden table in the garden of my dear friends Tina and Arina.

'Adieu, notre petite table,' I sang to cheer myself up as I passed yards which, now that they had no fences, merged indistinguishably with the road. The asphalt was cracked and bulging, bursting with roots and with withered grasses that had swelled in the rain.

In the evening we sat around the garden table under the blossoming lilacs and I had to tell everyone all about Paris – about my studies and the exhibitions and my *p'tit déj* of coffee and a croissant, sitting on one of those café chairs that face outwards onto the street like seats in a cinema. Our guests were thrilled.

'Bet you were in Les Deux Magots,' they said, 'in Saint-Germain-des-Prés.'

'Yes,' I said, not wanting to disappoint them. Yes, of course I was.

But although their interest was genuine and their questions so heartfelt that I gave a lively account of myself, I began to feel depressed again, uncomfortable about the way we were saying 'there' and 'here at home'. Was I actually *here at home* anywhere these days?

Then a flock of wall creepers flew up, their tiny bodies quivering with those rolling Rs.

'The wall creepers!' our friends called out. 'Can you hear them? They do sing beautifully. We ought to drink to them. Where have you hidden the champagne? Did anyone remember to put it to cool?'

I only felt tired and miserable.

Later, at dusk, bats flew out of the abandoned half-built houses – so many that they sounded like a babbling river. They streaked past us one by one, agitated, unsettling, veering off at sharp angles only to shoot out again somewhere else.

Margot and the others laughed. 'Ooh,' they squealed when a bat flew near their faces – and they seemed to enjoy themselves like old times as they remembered older times still.

I told myself I'd leave the next day. I would say I had urgent business in Paris.

The scream – that famous blood-curdling scream – woke me that very night. Margot and the guests would later claim that they too had woken and looked out, but when I started up in bed, all was calm. The shadow of the fence lay motionless; even the fir trees were still, and a heaviness lay over the world, as if the moonlight had smothered everything – our flowers, the rutted asphalt, the roadside scrub, the pale, half-finished buildings in the neighbours' gardens.

I stood at the open window, looking out to see if I could spot whatever was trying to force itself upon us. It seemed to me that I could distinguish every stalk and blade of grass in the bright moonlight, even the lines I had scored into the wooden gate as a child – and after a while, a scratching sound reached me, or perhaps its echo, and I listened.

'Come on,' I said. 'Come out so I can see you.'

Still nothing moved. There was only the rushing of the river on the other side of the forest, a steady flow of stillness.

Quickly I turned my head to catch a glimpse of this thing.

It retreated, lurking out of sight.

If only I could see it, I thought, I might be less scared.

I turned my head again. I wasn't going to let it creep around unseen any more.

'Come on! Come here!'

And then all at once I saw it. I was leaning out to close the shutters and it scuttled past me on its way down from the roof – an almost human creature climbing down the wall on all fours, head first like a lizard.

It was clothed in black so that my eyes were drawn to its white hands, the long, pale fingers curled like claws. I banged with the flat of my hand against the windowpane and when it turned I recognised it.

'You?'

It looked at me challengingly and I shouted, 'Shoo!' to scare it off like an animal, but it clung to the wall and twisted its face into a lascivious smile.

It looked as if it might pounce.

Then all of a sudden it wriggled away and I thought I saw it vanish into a small crack in the ground.

High up, under the roof, our yellow wax lamp was burning. Unusually, there were no moths flying about. Nothing stirred.

All was still again.

I closed the window, noisily, but remained standing there for some time. Now, though, instead of looking out, I was staring into the reflecting windowpane at myself sitting there, hands in lap with the room behind me, imagining all kinds of impossible things.

IV

The Fall

OUR WALK IN THE MOUNTAINS was the result of a spur-of-the-moment decision. For two days I had sat on the balcony drawing the mountain peaks in blue haze; it was time I saw something else. I remember Margot saying that she might not be an expert, but it seemed to her almost as if my wild pencil strokes were an attempt to impose on nature my own view of it – a dramatic, Victorian view. We laughed.

How I'd love to have had Mamargot's view of things, her gentle, sometimes distracted manner.

At times it bothered me that I was so different; I saw it as a betrayal of her.

There were no signposted paths leading from B. – or none that we knew of – so it was up to us to find a good route.

'En bonne compagnie nous marchons sur les plus beaux chemins,' someone said, and we recognised the quotation from I've forgotten where. One of the women objected that we didn't have suitable shoes, but that only made for more hilarity – we would just have to take the arms of our gallant friends.

And so we sallied forth, a cheerful, noisy crew, the gentlemen in jackets and straw hats and the ladies in elegant dresses and, for the most part, silk stockings and dainty indoor shoes – though I was barelegged and wore sandals. I have a vivid memory of those sandals, as if they were in some way important: they were comfortable strap sandals in old rose by Comme des Garçons. I'd bought a second pair for Mamargot, in royal blue.

Mamargot squeezed my arm and pointed at our friends. 'Look! Wouldn't they make a lovely painting?'

That day Yunus was also one of the party – an Iraqi friend of Geo and a tenant of one of his Bucharest flats. Geo introduced him to us in glowing tones: Yunus was the son he'd never had, a good lad, a promising doctor. Then he launched into a story about how at Yunus's graduation ceremony, before the mortarboard throwing, a band had struck up 'Gaudeamus igitur', and Yunus, believing that they were playing the Romanian national anthem, had solemnly put his hand on his heart. We snorted with laughter and then, of course, tried to stifle it, so as not to embarrass Yunus. But he laughed too and put his hand on his heart again – and Geo said, 'See why I love him? He's a true patriot.'

I remember being struck by Yunus's gleaming black hair and the rather antediluvian fringe that he flicked out of his eyes with a toss of his head. He was so shy in my presence that I circled him with theatrical nonchalance as we walked, sometimes getting closer to him, sometimes falling behind with Margot or going on ahead with Geo's wife Dominica – known affectionately to us as Ninel – and her mother Madame Didina. This last was a cousin of Margot. She had the same upright posture and aristocratic tilt of the head, so that when I think of her now it is her prominent jaw that I remember and her nearly closed eyes.

We chatted and laughed, and I could regale you with a number of anecdotes that were told on that walk, but it would distract you from the real story – and in any case the outing was dominated somewhat by Geo and his tirade against the country's corrupt politicians – a torrent of words only intermittently broken by the ladies' attempt to lighten the mood.

Geo spoke vociferously about the unconscionable nomenklatura, especially the old mayor of B. and his son who had recently taken over from him. I took his arm as he spoke, and listened to him.

'Yes,' I said, 'I know,' or: 'I didn't know that.'

And he ranted on about how they'd embezzled EU funds for the weaving mill to buy the Ceaușescus' 'protocol' house with its indoor pool and tennis courts – *and* the old hotel and three restaurants on the road to Brașov. They also owned the transport company that ran the local bus service – that was why the trains no longer stopped in B. The whole thing had been rigged by him and his party cronies.

I'd come on a bus from Bucharest, hadn't I? *Well then!* And what about the plans for a rubbish dump? That was another scam they'd cooked up for their own benefit.

Geo proceeded to list all the crooked deals he knew of in B., huffing and snorting and asking us questions which he immediately answered himself.

'A rubbish dump in B.? Come on. They're not stupid. First they bought the land for it, then they sold it back to the state at five times the original price. Then they hustled up state project funds through some dodgy company run by the in-laws, and now every taxpayer here is charged for rubbish disposal, though no rubbish truck has ever made it anywhere near B. Of course not! Why would they send round rubbish trucks when we've all the countryside to dump rubbish in? The corruptos, of course, blame the state of the roads – say they need repairing first. And guess what, they just happen to have their own construction firm all lined up for the job.'

'We know all this, Geo,' Mamargot said. 'Don't get so worked up.'

'Remember what the priest said on Sunday,' Madame Didina urged him.

'Yes, that was a very good sermon,' Mamargot said – I *must* hear this man preach sometime.

And she pulled me to her side and gave me a detailed rendition of the sermon, in a voice loud enough for everyone to hear.

I will quote it here for her sake, because she was so anxious to tell me about it.

It might come as a surprise to us, the priest had said, to find those we'd despised in this life standing so close to the throne of God in the hereafter. But who were we to judge?

It was a sermon about the Pharisee and the publican – the Romanians of our days, as the priest put it.

The Pharisee is a man of good standing and reputation, tastefully dressed, well-educated, but quite capable of swindling the publican if he stands to gain by it. Deceive the deceiver, he tells himself, and you cancel out the deceit.

The publican is a terrible pleb who profits from every regime. Maybe in the past he collaborated with the Communist dictatorship; now, all these years on, he's still on the side of the powers that be. Everything for him is about making money – creaming it off, raking it in.

And both men go to pray.

The Pharisee stands by himself and thanks God he's not like other people – an extortioner or an unjust man, or even a man like the publican.

But the publican stands at a distance, won't so much as raise his eyes; instead he beats his breast and prays, 'God be merciful to me a sinner!'

So which of them was the better person?

'Well?' Margot looked at me expectantly. 'The publican, of course! Doesn't it say, *Every one that exalteth himself shall be abased; and he that humbleth himself shall be exalted*?'

Geo snorted. Did the publican leave off his bad ways after that humble prayer of his? And wouldn't *he*, Geo, an *artist*, be better off looking out for himself and thinking about his own soul rather than getting worked up about other people? Was it really so noble to look the other way? Didn't society suffer from the indifference of those who had the nous to judge the situation?

'Oh Geo,' Mamargot sighed. 'We all suffer. And some day, very soon, we will die.'

I squeezed Mamargot's arm and felt her return the pressure. From the front of the group Ninel called out that she had some chocolates in her bag – did anyone fancy a chocolate?

Someone, I seem to remember, was in the middle of one of those bear and rabbit jokes, but Geo came back to my side and, ignoring Margot, insisted on explaining to me how the elections were won: it was all rigged – there were documentaries about it – though God knows why they bothered; Romania had been in a Sleeping Beauty slumber for years.

'Isn't that what it says in the first verse of the national anthem: *Awake, Romanian, from your sleep of death*. But when's it going to happen? When are we going to wake up?'

'Yes, when will Geo's wife finally wake up?' called Ninel, who was now at the back of our little procession. This joke was new to me, but it made the others laugh.

'Oh, children,' Madame Didina called, 'Wouldn't you rather tell me what kind of bird that is that I can hear?'

But Geo was not to be distracted. He told us that the corruptos had also helped themselves to woodland, marking off so and so many acres with electric netting to make themselves a private hunting ground. It beggared belief, he said. They'd even diverted the river, which now flowed through 'their' hunting ground. And they'd dug a lake for fishing – that, too, for private use, of course.

Madame Didina said that Geo's jittery tone was making her nervous – also, she was upset by some of the things he was saying, especially the *way* he was saying them, as if we were all to blame for other people's racketeering.

And Mamargot said, 'Forgive me, Geo, but you complain about the nomenklatura and then speak just like them.'

'We came out to admire and be happy,' Madame Didina said.

As she spoke, I looked up and saw little flies gleaming in the shafts of light, and noticed that there were woodpeckers knocking on the trees overhead and further along the path. Someone said it was amazing that the little things didn't damage their brains, banging away at the wood like that – apparently they closed their eyes when they were hammering and chipping, to protect themselves from flying sawdust.

We went on in this vein for some time and no longer talked of other things.

Our little group shimmered in the glinting light – at every gust of wind it looked as if we all jumped in the air at once, while somewhere below us, the river made a rushing sound, as if to soothe our anxiety and fears. *Sh-sh-sh*...

It must have been the newly diverted river – it hadn't been there in the past. Or was it just that I'd never been on this particular path before? I can't say for sure. There were no signposts – only the occasional cross on the slope. After a while, though, these crosses came thick and fast. They were memorial crosses for fallen hikers; one of them, I remember, bore the inscription, *Travel well, stranger. My journey ends here.*

We crossed ourselves and one of the ladies said, 'Oh dear,' which made us laugh so much that we had to stop and rest.

How can I explain? It was like a shudder going through us; we were racked by uncontrollable laughter. We laughed the way we used to laugh at *Zitti, zitti* and at the guests on the balcony pointing at the dark-red river and pretending to be Moses unleashing the first plague.

We laughed with open mouths and, looking at the others, we saw that they were laughing too. Even Geo was laughing now; we were all laughing together at last, roaring with laughter, gasping for breath, laughing tears. The slope was steep at this point; with every step we took, we had to wedge our feet between the jutting roots to find a foothold. So there we were, laughing away on that steep slope, leaning against the damp rockface in our finery and staring down into the abyss, in whose depths, beneath the rising mist, the river rushed along.

When we stopped laughing, it was quiet, and the river was suddenly so loud that it sounded as if it were about to rip the narrow path, roots and all, from under our feet. From this point in the story, I may muddle up the order of events – partly, perhaps, because no order really seems to make sense to me.

I resume writing here, after considerable doubts about my ability to tell this story led me to interrupt my work for a while. I had begun to doubt my memory. And it became clear to me that I hadn't been paying attention at the time – or not, at any rate, to the events I have taken it upon myself to relate.

I had thought this was *my* story, simply because it happened to *me*. In fact, its being mine could also imply a certain responsibility, a duty assigned to me at some long-forgotten point in time.

Countless times I have read over what I wrote about muddling up the order of events because no order really seems to make sense. Now, though, I have the impression that the opposite is the case and that *any* order makes sense, because it's not a matter of cause and effect, but of fate.

Yet isn't that precisely what I was trying to dispute – the crippling notion that we are all subject to fate and powerless to defy it?

I have been through another tortuously long period of what I feared would prove invincible lethargy. *I can't begin to describe it. How can I possibly write about it* ... But I have made up my mind: I will write the way I can. I will write as if I were painting a scene on a wall, a Wallachian fresco with a certain daemon in the middle.

There we were, then, high on the narrow path, afraid to move. Down below, the river rushed along, and we shivered with damp as much as fear. I seem to remember that we said nothing for a long time, but then we began to talk quickly – a lot of nonsense and silly jokes. That crude joke about the bear who wipes his bum with little animals and ends up reaching for the hedgehog. Someone burst into tears. And there was an argument too, though I've forgotten who argued or what they argued about – some trifle or other. I could, of course, surmise that it was because of this argument that Madame Didina turned away, but that would be to assign blame where there is no blame to assign. Madame Didina simply slipped, as any of us might have done.

She fell and she fell. I saw her, very small in the distance, rolling head-over-heels down the hill before she vanished into the ground mist.

V

The Tomb on the Hill

MISS SANDA OPENED ALL the windows in the house and all the doors, and she covered all the mirrors with black sheets. She lit and relit candles that kept going out in the draught.

Some of the old peasant men who were still in B. dropped by to offer their condolences; they twisted their caps in their hands and drank sullenly to the deceased. A motley parade of women showed up too – all strangers to me, but full of affection for us in their grief. Among them was a shrivelled old dame no one recognised, who tore her headscarf from her head in the middle of the drawing room to reveal a shock of magenta hair which she proceeded to pull out in clumps. 'Didina! Dina!' she wailed hoarsely. 'Where have you gone, my soul? In whose hands are you leaving us?'

While Ninel and Geo and even some of our less permanent guests suffered the damp-faced embraces of these teary strangers and began to weep with them themselves, you could tell that Margot was embarrassed by the formal visits, though she was prepared to submit to them with that gentle understanding that comes to those who face last things.

Atanasie – or Ata, as we used to call him – also came to pay his respects, dressed all in black – black waistcoat, black trousers, black dinner jacket with silk lapels. Miss Sanda presented him with the silver tray of hors d'oeuvres and was earnestly explaining the canapés to him when someone reached a hand over the tray – 'Delighted, delighted!' – and sent everything flying. I saw Ata refuse all offers to help clean his jacket. Then he looked about him, white napkin in hand – and our eyes met.

He came over to me at once, kissed my hand and offered his condolences. He said something nice like, 'May God give her a place among the just.' Then he looked at my cleavage.

'Did I give you that cross?' he asked.

'Don't think so,' I said.

I couldn't imagine why he thought the small crucifix on my chain was from him. Maybe he'd once given all the girls in B. crosses and was now a little hazy about the details. I couldn't work out what it was about this thought that made me feel so hurt.

'Our lady from Paris,' someone said at my side. It was Sabin Voicu, Ata's father and the former mayor.

He gave me a smacking kiss on each cheek, hugged me and sighed.

'Don't weep for the old,' he said. 'It's the way of all flesh.'

If he could help in any way, he was here for us.

'Thank you,' I said, avoiding using his name, because although he'd been mayor all through my childhood and youth, and was much spoken of, I wasn't sure which of his names was his surname – whether, that is, he was Sabin Voicu or Voicu Sabin. On the hoardings and in the media it was written sometimes one way, sometimes the other, and people talking about him also alternated between Mr Sabin and Mr Voicu.

Sabin Voicu or Voicu Sabin – he even switched between the two when introducing himself. As I'm afraid he's going to feature quite heavily in my report and I don't want him confusing you as well, I shall, for simplicity's sake, stick to Sabin. If Sabin's name was elusive, his appearance was unforgettable. I think any portrait painter would have regarded him as a worthy model: everything about him was so extreme that he seemed to wear even his deepest secrets on his face, with more than a hint of tragedy in his expression. He embraced his son, closing his eyes as if he, too, needed his condolences. Then the two of them set off through the crowd of mourners – the young man with the gelled-back black hair and the striking aquiline nose, and the small, rotund man whose shiny bald pate was plastered with a long strand of hair.

Once, in my childhood, I saw a gust of wind catch that fraudulent strand that Sabin grew above his left ear and carefully plastered to his head. It stood up in the air in the shape of a sickle.

Now I watched Ata. He greeted everyone aloofly, then made a quick exit, while his father lingered.

Sabin's snivelling voice rose above the general buzz. 'Dreadful, dreadful,' he was saying to Ninel, 'we all have to be very brave,' and: 'We have to carry on somehow.'

Even Geo had to submit to being hugged and clapped on the shoulder – there was no escaping Sabin's smug compassion.

'If there's anything I can do, you must tell me. You really must. We've known each other so long. Age makes you sentimental.'

He was sweating, and that long strand of hair had slipped over his forehead – a pitiful sight.

At one point I spotted him coming out of the kitchen. He announced solemnly that he was going out in the garden for a moment; he'd be right back. He was always on his way in or out, making himself useful everywhere – and whenever he passed me, panting and sweating, he would say, 'No weeping for the old, now.'

Each time, I found myself almost thanking him for his words, his officiousness – for the way he acted as if he were master of the house. He lit candles, then bustled off again to fetch all the wine from the cellar so that we could drink to the deceased. He also brought with him a stuffed squirrel. 'Look who I found down there. Cheeky little fellow!'

Ninel took the squirrel in her arms, and several of our friends began to reminisce about changing the furniture in Villa Diana.

'It was Diana, wasn't it?'

'Diana, yes, had you forgotten?'

How young they'd been in those days and what fun they'd had. Madame Didina had been good fun, too,

God bless her, waving her cigarette around and cheating at cards – there'd been no one like her!

Sabin poured sour cherry liqueur and Muscat Ottonel from Geo's vineyards into whatever glasses people happened to have in front of them, even shot glasses, and we ate cozonac from Capșa: the kind with lots of nuts and the kind with Turkish delight. There were also cheese and mushroom mille-feuilles made by Miss Sanda.

'The gold-edged plates have been counted, just so you know,' she hissed at the old women, and we talked at length and animatedly about our lovely memories, interrupted only by those same old women from B. who were wailing more softly now – and only between canapés. 'Oh Didina,' they sighed, 'my little soul, in whose hands are you leaving us?'

'Awful,' Sabin said. 'The good times are over and we're all getting old … Only Mrs Margot doesn't get old,' he said, clapping Mamargot on the shoulder. Had she noticed, he asked, that everyone else had moved their fences out four metres into the forest years ago and that hers was the only one in its original position? He'd turn a blind eye, she knew that – he could even send someone along to do it for her. He could find workmen to do her another tennis court, too. Margot nodded and let him top her up, and then Sabin did the rounds again, filling everyone's glasses to the brim. He finished with his own and then hurried to be the first to reach out of the window and pour out a drop to the soul of the deceased. I think I saw tears in his eyes.

Meanwhile, the deceased was laid out in the room next door, a chilly little box room off the passage leading to the back stairs. I peeped inside. The boxes had been tidied away. Madame Didina's mortal remains lay on a child's bed under a white sheet and bore little resemblance to the shape of a body. On a small table next to the bed, a red candle was burning.

It had been decided that Madame Didina should be buried in the cemetery of B., in the ancestral vault. Margot hadn't been there for some time and was no longer sure which members of the family were buried there and whether there was any space, so she took a small sack with her for any bones that might need moving.

Apart from Geo and Ninel, who had taken their cars to the next town to pick up the priest and his deacon, and a few friends who would be arriving later on the bus from Bucharest, we all went on foot to the cemetery: the family, our guests and Miss Sanda with her dustpan and brush and a bucket full of cloths. Even Sabin joined us; from the way he went on, you'd have thought no grave in the cemetery could be found without him. He was accompanied by a small gypsy with a large mallet.

You could see the cemetery from the first bend in the road, up on the right, behind the tall oaks. I hadn't realised it was there; I'd always thought the grey specks were flocks of sheep, when in fact they were old vaults and gravestones with marble statues and ornate cast-iron crosses, everything half-covered in ivy, tall grasses and bushes.

There were no paths in this cemetery; it stretched up the hill to a small wood and you trampled your own path between the graves.

We walked from vault to vault, reading names and years if they were legible. Mamargot thought she recognised some of the family names – that of her godparents, for example, the people who had owned the grand house with the acacia wood where she was allowed to ride as a girl.

'Look what an impressive cemetery this is,' Sabin said proudly. 'We could be in Bucharest or Paris. Who says B.'s only a village?'

Then we found it – a beautiful marble vault with long glassless windows.

'I should send my men up here,' Sabin said. 'They make stained glass like in an Italian cathedral.'

But Mamargot only said, 'Yes, very nice,' and ran her hand over the weathered green marble wall with the inscriptions.

'Take a look at this,' Sabin began, as if he were our tour guide. 'There are graves here from 1764 and 1490 – even one from 1477. Just think: 1477! Who says we have no history here in B.?'

We almost felt like laughing again.

'A friend of mine from Switzerland tells me that over there you have to rent graves for your dead, and after twenty years that's it: they chuck them out and scatter the bones in the next graves along. No one there has ancestors from 1477 in the family grave – not even the Einsteins.'

There was a loud creak from a water pump. Miss Sanda was filling the bucket.

'To work!' Sabin yelled with gusto, rolling up his shirtsleeves.

Three of our friends helped us lift the heavy marble slab by its iron rings and heave it aside. A corner broke off, but Sabin said it could be repaired. 'On we go!'

They lowered a ladder into the vault, and the small gypsy climbed down with a torch. He returned a moment later and told us there were three burial niches on the left, one above the other, and three on the right; another three on either side further back and two gravestones let into the floor at the far end.

But what was on the slabs that closed the niches? Were there inscriptions? What did they say? Mamargot must have been wondering the same as me.

'He can't read,' Sabin said brightly. One of the family would have to climb down with him.

Mamargot asked me to go and open one of the older graves; she gave me the small sack for the bones.

So down I went into the vault after the gypsy. As I went, I heard Sabin say that the 'little guy' was great, he'd vouch for him any day. If we liked, he could let us have him for a time, to light the candles in the vault and do a bit of sweeping. But Margot said Miss Sanda could do that, and even as she spoke I heard a swishing sound that surely came from Miss Sanda's broom. Then I reached the ground, and the noise of my footsteps drowned out the voices above.

The small gypsy gave me the torch and I examined the stone slabs on the wall; the grave at the bottom on the right was from 1490 and said *Ecaterina Fronius Siegel*.

'Would you knock open this lower grave, please,' I said.

'Low I can do,' the small gypsy said and I felt almost sorry for finding that funny.

As a little light reached him from the hole we had come in by, I took the torch and went to inspect the other graves. They were all old; the most recent was that of Raluca Marie Filipescu, 1782–1849, presumably a grandmother or great-grandmother – there was an Antoine Filipescu in our vault in Bellu Cemetery in Bucharest, who had died at a much later date. I also examined the two graves in the floor: first the stone on the left, so warped by the damp as to be illegible, and then that on the right. Meanwhile the gypsy chipped away at the bottom grave with rhythmic blows, filling the vault with a cold dust that seemed to make everything brighter and yet at the same time more obscure.

There I stood, then, suspecting nothing, looking down at the grave that was to become so famous.

The white dust billowed out in the dim light of the torch, and I had to stoop to make out anything on the ledger stone. When I did see something, I started back and must have let out a sound that was heard by the gypsy.

Some of you will be familiar with the image on the ledger stone – I, too, know it better after seeing photoshopped versions of it in the media, with enhanced brightness and contrast. When I first saw it in the vault, I couldn't really make sense of what I was looking at; in fact, I thought the engraving showed something quite different: two mating dogs, the male on all fours on top of the bitch, their spasming bodies forming a ring closed

59

at both ends – heads as well as genitals, because the dog's jaws were clamped on the bitch's neck.

Those of you familiar with the picture will know that it can also be read another way and actually shows a dragon vanquishing a lion, the Ordo Draconis.

'Ata must see this,' the small gypsy said, and I realised he was standing next to me. 'He'll want a tattoo of it, like the Italians.'

I went back to the wall of niches with the torch and told him to get on with his work.

He followed me and hammered at the grave a few times, and a brick wall appeared beneath the layer of cement, the bricks loosely stacked so that they could be pulled out like drawers. The gypsy set a few bricks aside to make space. Then he stood before me with a brick in one hand; the open grave behind him came up to his armpits, and he asked whimsically if I thought we should also look for jewellery in the grave. He didn't even say 'jewellery', but smiled rapturously and said, 'jewels!'

'What's that?' I asked. He repeated his question, and a laugh went through me like a shudder. I couldn't help myself – I opened my mouth and roared with laughter.

'Say that again, please,' I gasped, leaning against the wall to catch my breath.

From outside someone called, 'Everything all right down there?'

By then I was sliding around on my knees, weeping with laughter. 'Say that again, please, I beg you.'

But the gypsy stood motionless, his eyes averted, the brick pressed to his chest.

'Hurry up, please,' a voice called down.

And others yelled out, 'Yes, get a move on, it's getting chilly up here.'

I was almost dizzy with laughter – and also, I suppose, from the air in the vault.

I went down on all fours and reached into the niche; on the stone floor of the grave I found some fragments of skeleton, a piece of skull, a few longer bones and some bone splinters. All these I gathered up and put in the sack along with four wrought-iron wing ornaments as big as a fist – presumably from the corners of coffins – and a pair of green silk shoes each with a purple stone and a small, coquettishly curved block heel. Did the ancestor buried here in 1490 really have such little feet, I wondered, or had the shoe shrunk to the size of a doll's shoe? Probably both. The shoes looked as good as new.

Later there was talk of green smoke, but I didn't see any – nor do I recall smelling anything much beside cold earth and dust.

Back outside I looked once more at the engraved names. Yes, the bones I had fetched out were those of Ecaterina Fronius Siegel.

At about midday we were at home again with our family and friends, many of whom I hadn't seen since childhood; we embraced warmly. My mother was there too, and the priest and his deacon arrived with Ninel who was, I remember, wearing a black lace dress with several flounces; she spoke softly and insistently to Geo, stroking his head and comforting him.

The air was steeped in incense and, in the billows of shimmering smoke, everyone moved more slowly than usual, peaceably.

The small sack of bones was on the drawing-room table, waiting to be blessed; later it would be placed in Madame Didina's grave. But when the priest began the blessing, and we all stood there crossing ourselves, our eyes on the sack, it occurred to me that the little wing ornaments were still in there – and the green shoes. I went up to the table, pushed aside the candlestick with the burning candle, grabbed the sack, took out the bits of wrought iron and the shoes, and put them back on the table next to the sack of bones. And just as the priest was saying the lovely prayer, 'O God of spirits and of all flesh, who hast trodden down death, and hast overcome the evil one—' Miss Sanda let out a series of bestial shrieks, a kind of porcine squealing or grunting which only gradually, when someone rushed over with a glass of water, became recognisable as words: 'The shoes! No shoes on the table!'

'To hell with your superstitions, Miss Sanda!' my mother shouted angrily – and then immediately apologised to the priest. 'That woman,' she said, 'lives in perpetual fear.'

It was true: Miss Sanda had brought every superstition in B. into our house – all manner of fears and constraints, which we had begun by observing in a spirit of anthropological inquiry, only to find ourselves increasingly controlled and restricted as the years went by.

As a teenager I had drawn up a list of Miss Sanda's ridiculous beliefs. *If you spill salt on the table, there will be a quarrel; you must pick it up and throw it over your shoulder. You should never pour water into partly filled glasses or cut a loaf at both ends – it brings no good. Open scissors bring unexpected conflict. Knives, too, should never be left blade uppermost.*

Taking the rubbish out after dark brings bad luck. Beating carpets or hanging out the washing after sunset is unlucky. So is putting up an umbrella in the house. Borrow a broom and you're in for a hiding. The same goes for breaking off part way through making the bed.

All this I blamed on Miss Sanda's fastidious house-keeping. But her superstitions extended even into the most mundane habits. *If you scratch your left ear or examine your nails, someone will soon be saying bad things about you. If your nose itches, you're due a beating. If you drop the comb while you're combing your hair, you'll soon have cause for tears. The same if you drop a knife, put your clothes on back-to-front or slip into a shirt left arm first. If you walk around with one shoe on and the other off, there will soon be a death. Ditto if you look at yourself in the mirror with a candle in your hand.*

Another thing you mustn't do is walk under ladders. Sanda was always taking the ladder down from the apple tree and laying it on the ground along the back fence.

You must always have lots of garlic in the house, preferably in braids. But you must never take garlic out at night, because it brings nothing but bad luck.

Sanda acted at all times as if she were warding off grave misfortune from us with small, precise gestures, so that it was with immense fascination that we watched her busy herself about the house – and in some cases with a sense of wonder verging on awe.

'This superstition must come from somewhere,' one of the guests would say. 'Maybe there's something in it.'

Even Mamargot began to say that although she wasn't the least bit superstitious, she was going to be very careful.

You must never put your slippers on backwards when you get out of bed in the morning. And you should never be the thirteenth person to enter a room.

When Mamargot left the house, she always went out through the same door she had come in at. This meant that the back door to the little kitchen garden was hardly used any more.

We no longer looked in the mirror in the evening, especially by candlelight, and we stopped cuttings our nails at night – and on Fridays and Saturdays. Throwing nail parings on the fire was unlucky, too, Sanda warned us, as was spitting in the fire.

The list grew longer and longer.

I resolved to look out my old notebook and add the superstition about shoes on the table.

VI

There's Somebody There

THIS TIME IT WAS THE STILLNESS that woke me, a stillness so complete that I was startled by my own movements. The big mirror to the right of the bed was gone; the bare wall seemed to have shifted closer. Moonlight shone onto the snowy white sheet, making it gleam. I grabbed the sheet and wrapped it round me, good and tight to calm my breathing.

I walked from room to room, looking for the furniture. It was all gone. The parquet was covered in grey rectangles – a memory game! Surely I ought to be able to remember what used to be there. How could I forget a thing like that?

I stared at a square shape near my bedroom door and started to rack my brains, then realised to my horror that I wasn't even sure it was actually the door to my room.

I was all alone. There was no one left to tell me stories about the past. Everything was over.

I cried soundlessly, feeling my forehead move. How long had I been asleep?

The parquet creaked; I wanted to hide. I was seized by panic at the thought that I was still here. I wasn't supposed to be here with everything gone.

The door to the stairs was lying on the floor; it was hard to open. I strained silently at the rings as scraping footsteps approached. Then I gave it a jerk and it opened a crack and I pushed my way through.

I knew these stairs well. I ran down them barefoot, gripping the banister which was all muddy. I slipped and fell in the mud, fell through roots and branches, tried to grab hold of something, but grasped only rotten leaves, and soon I was slipping again, faster now, first over scree, then over ivy and grass, my body all twisted.

Then someone said, 'Shhh,' very close by. Perhaps it was me, not yet dead, going on my way up the road under the bright moon.

I knew I mustn't turn my back on the house. But how did I know? I walked sideways, crossing my feet, and at every third step I jumped. I felt the cold air from the forest behind me and heard that soft scratching sound under the bark of the trees, but: Not now, I told myself, not now. I counted my steps: one-two-jump, one-two-jump.

Soon I'd got into the rhythm and could dance more quickly, the way I should. I mustn't let anything stop me.

I pretended I couldn't hear him – that I hadn't noticed he was following me.

He was coming after me up the hill, clumping along unsteadily, as if he were tripping over a long cloak.

If I could just manage to keep up the rhythm!

I beat out the time to myself with little whimpering sounds. I knew I mustn't look back, not even if he called me.

I tried not to listen, but I heard him calling me all the same – in old-fashioned, almost dulcet tones.

The scrape and clack of his shoes, the little footsteps coming nearer and nearer.

Then I saw his shoes—

He was wearing women's shoes!

The green shoes from the vault!

I felt his cold grip on my wrist before he twisted my arm, then his cold buttons pressing between my shoulder blades, his hot breath on my throat. I leaned my head back against his shoulder and he gently returned the pressure.

There we stood, leaning against one another, yearning.

But why did I start to scream?

Someone held my mouth shut and said, 'Shhh!'

It was Yunus, who was lying beside me.

He smoothed my wet hair off my forehead. Would I like him to bring me a glass of water?

'No, please don't. The floorboards creak.'

Then would I like to hear something funny? 'Another military service story?'

I nodded.

'All right,' he said, cheerfully, and I sat up in bed, the big pillow at the small of my back.

As he told the story, I looked about the room, trying to memorise the layout: to my left, the big oak wardrobe with the wooden chest next to it; in the corner opposite, the two armchairs and the little card table; over by the window, my easel, with grass sticking to its legs; above it, the gilt-framed painting by Arthur Verona, like a second window looking out over a green meadow with two reclining shepherd boys; to my right, the big mirror, and above me, over the bed, on the east wall – I couldn't see them, but I knew they were there – the icons and the little oil lamp that was always lit.

Yunus told me that when he'd gone for his military medical he had claimed to be unfit for service, but was then deemed so fit that he was sent to the paratroopers. He was seventeen at the time – all the paratroopers were seventeen, and they were all afraid to jump. They clung on for dear life at the door of the training aircraft, so that a small sturdy guy had to fly out with them, just to push them down.

'How?' I asked Yunus.

'Like this,' he said, pretending to push me, but then holding me tight again, even tighter than before.

'Didn't feel a thing,' I said.

He laughed and pushed me again to make me cling to him. Instead I pushed him back so hard that he fell out of bed with a crash. We both said, 'Shhh' and laughed softly.

Why hadn't he opened his parachute, I asked.

But he stood up and said, 'Revenge,' making the word sound so comical, so awkwardly foreign that I felt moved to help him. We needn't go into the details of what followed, because you can all imagine it – or can you? In the rapture of memory, I am inclined to think you probably can't.

At dawn I asked Yunus for another story and he began to describe his military incursion into Kuwait.

'Okay, listen,' he said brightly.

One day, the young paratroopers' plane maintained its speed for longer than usual. At first they thought it was because of bad weather, but the sky was clear. They were wrapped up warm for the jump training, so they were all sweating, and one of them threw up on Yunus's uniform. But the captain said nothing the whole time and wouldn't let them speak among themselves.

After two hours, he passed round a handout showing pencil sketches of men's faces: oval heads with and without beards, with and without moustaches, and with a snazzy selection of head dresses, head bands, kofias and sunglasses.

'As you can see,' the captain said, 'all these pictures are of the same man. He is in disguise. I want you to remember what he looks like and, God willing, arrest him immediately if you get the chance.'

It turned out that the villain was the king of Kuwait, from whom the Iraqis were to liberate the enslaved brotherhood.

'If you catch him on the run from his people, you must disarm him without fail.'

('Like Ceaușescu!' Yunus said, and laughed.)

Then the boys were pushed out one by one. Once in the air, they were supposed to count to ten before they pulled their rip cords. But, as usual, they counted 'one-two-ten' very fast and then pulled them immediately, so that the small plane lurched under the force of the opening parachutes.

Yunus was the last to jump. 'Watch out for donkeys,' were the captain's last words to him.

Down on the ground the small group was equipped with old bayonet rifles and sent on foot through Kuwait City where they were to join up with a larger troop. They were shown a map, but weren't allowed to take it with them; everything had to be committed to memory. It was all quite straightforward, Yunus said; he still remembered the route: down King Fahad Street as far as King Khalid Bin Abdulaziz, then a right turn up Abdulaziz Bin Abdulrahman Al Saud until they met the others.

The trouble was that when they arrived in the city, the place was mayhem. They got caught up in the morning rush-hour traffic – in a roar of engines and a blast of horns that echoed strangely off the tall glass buildings.

None of them had been abroad before and they peered about them and stared at the tall buildings until one of them spotted the three water towers – a famous landmark! – and they decided to change their route.

This was, perhaps, a mistake, but the directions they'd been given wouldn't have got them to the meeting place anyway. There were no pavements in that part of the city and no people except in cars; Yunus and his little group were the only ones on foot, out in the blazing sun, the dust, the exhaust fumes.

What could they do? One of them walked out onto the road and tried to stop a car, but it sped past without slowing down.

Maybe they should take off the thick clothes they were wearing under their uniforms? Not on the street, Yunus said – that was no way for soldiers to behave when they were on a mission. Later! Very soon! And the more piteously the men complained of thirst and tiredness, the firmer he became.

Around midday someone stopped at last – a taxi driver. He wound down his window and music blared out: *Ya habibi, ya habibi* – the wailing voice of Umm Kulthum. *Oh, my friend.*

Dazed by the music, the driver smiled at the soldiers and said, still in the world of Umm Kulthum, 'Ya habibi!' He was an old man in a crumpled dishdasha, a dented kofia on his head.

'Peace be with you, brother,' Yunus said. 'Glad you've stopped. We've come to liberate you and we need some help.'

The driver turned down the music.

'Ahlan u-sahlan, welcome! Who are you?'

'Iraqi soldiers,' Yunus said, and his colleagues slapped the shafts of their rifles with newfound pride.

'Ah, mashallah, bravo, bravo! And where are you from?'

'Iraq,' said one of the young men, amused.

'Ah, Iraq,' the old man cried in delight, as if something had suddenly become clear.

'Yes, brother, that's what we said,' Yunus told him.

'Ahlan u-sahlan,' the taxi driver said. 'Welcome, welcome!'

Yunus heard his men sigh and began to fear their impatience. They were standing in the shade of a tall glass tower, but it was hot and dusty, and they smelt of sweat and puke.

'Jannah, the Garden of Eden, is in Iraq,' the taxi driver said, indefatigable.

'That is correct, brother. But right now we're here and we're in a bit of a hurry.'

'Yes, that's right, habibi, you wanted to liberate me,' the man said joyfully.

'Indeed.'

'But who do you want to liberate me from?'

'From the tyrant, brother, the tyrant,' Yunus said impatiently.

'Ya habibi, my friend, I know only one tyrant,' the taxi driver yelled, putting his foot to the floor. 'My wife!'

And the small group of Iraqi soldiers watched in bewilderment as the taxi moved away, the driver leaning out of the window to yell back at them: 'It's my fate, brothers, I'm sorry! There's no escape!'

VII

A Nasty Discovery

MADAME DIDINA'S FUNERAL was held the next morning. The priest said the mass in our little church in B., a fifteenth-century chapel with a wide, overhanging roof, the walls intricately painted inside and out in the Byzantine style in many shades of blue: pale blue, grey blue, green blue, midnight blue. Azure blue Mary's heavenly mantle; blue the wilderness of miracles. and the burning bush; ethereal blue the handsomely draped togas of the ancient philosophers, precursors of Christianity like Sophocles, Plato, Aristoteles, Pythagoras. Blue, too, the prophetess Sibyl in the vineyard; blue the grapes, blue the pitchers by the well; blue the sea on which Peter walks in fear. Blue the distance; blue the foreground – the idle crowd looking on in apathy at the cruel torment; blue the angels' wings; blue the cloaks of the just on the slanting ladder to heaven; blue and wan the sinners tumbling into hell, pulled down by a deep-blue devil.

Blue, too, was the light that fell through the side windows and mingled with the incense as the priest said the prayers of forgiveness.

Madame Didina's mortal remains lay on the bier at the front of the church, covered in a white cloth; on top, about where her hands must have lain folded, was an icon of the Assumption. We had, as the priest observed, given her the same icon that was painted above the entrance to the church.

'The same icon,' Margot kept saying to the assembled company. 'It's the same icon.'

'It's my favourite,' I told her and she squeezed my hand gratefully.

On the icon, the Mother of God lies stretched out before the weeping apostles, while her Son, who has appeared unnoticed, solemnly cradles her soul in his arms in the form of a babe in swaddling clothes.

I will say no more about the mass for Madame Didina, and I would ask you not to expect me to talk of our grief either – or indeed any aspect of our shock at the sudden death, or the guilt and worry that plagued us. Such things should not be aired in public. That is my opinion, and more importantly, it is Margot's.

'Incroyable, l'indiscrétion de la mort,' Margot had said only that morning as she lit the red candle on the breakfast table.

'Emil Cioran!' the guests had promptly yelled.

And many had added, 'How true!'

Were we aloof? Unfeeling? Just because the local people would later express their grief and fears with such tireless energy, that is no reason to assume that their emotions were stronger or fiercer than ours – 'authentic', as some reports had it – or that the story should be told exclusively from their point of view, with their cranked-up pathos.

Should we, too, have been questioned? I don't know. But I have observed that there is a tendency these days to accept noisily expressed feelings as the truth, while being suspicious of introspection. Perhaps you will agree with me.

When the priest invited us to give Madame Didina a final kiss, we all kissed her through the white cloth. I kissed the stiff crease at the top, taking care not to flatten it, and the others, I think, did the same. Only Miss Sanda, I noticed, took a different approach, sobbing loudly and stooping almost into the coffin for the kiss. Touching a dead body brings good luck, she had said.

The priest struck up the Memory Eternal and we all joined in, swaying our bodies a little: 'Memory eternal, memory eternal'. Geo's baritone sounded so beautiful together with the priest's that it brought tears to our eyes.

Then, when the service was over, the coffin was carried out and lifted onto a horse-drawn hearse that Sabin had somehow managed to foist on us.

Geo led the way with the wooden cross, followed by the priest swinging the censer by its long chains hung with bells. Behind them came the hearse, and we brought up the rear.

We passed the houses I knew so well: Baba Lia's house, then the house of the three Gruia boys who had taught me how to mow with a scythe, then the grand house covered in ivy. Baba Lia used to sell borsht and there were always children playing in her courtyard, knocking over the borsht bottles with a great clatter. Now only the walls of the house remained; the roof had caved in. The Gruias' house was overshadowed by a high concrete wall, and the shutters were down. Only the grand house looked as fresh as ever; it was generally rented by a friend of Margot who stayed there with her two grandchildren – she had an unusual name but it has slipped my mind.

We used to make big bonfires in the courtyard of the ivy-covered house. It had originally belonged to Margot's friend's grandparents and then, like ours, been sold by public auction. Every summer, this friend would tap away at the walls with a little hammer, searching for the gold coins her grandfather had surely hidden there.

On one occasion this woman came to us quite distraught, laughing and crying at once. She had inadvertently knocked a hole in the wall and needed the discreet loan of a bucket of mortar and white lime. Help came in the end from the widow who lived next door to her – the mother of my rhyming friends Tina and Arina.

I loved spending time with Tina and Arina. They had a yard at the side of their house where they kept Bantams whose peeping chicks were a regular source of wonder. One year, we decorated Easter eggs in their garden, and I learnt how to make plant dyes and paint intricate patterns on the eggs. Now, as the funeral procession passed, there were low pink clouds shimmering over their garden.

As I walked with the other mourners, I felt that I was paying a last tribute not only to Madame Didina, but to the whole region. What a lot of memories I had of this place – and how long ago it all was.

Margot was so much older now, and I felt guilty towards her for harking back to my childhood and dwelling so fondly on the years of tyranny. Those were the years I meant when I talked about the things we *used to* do, whereas when Margot spoke of the way things *used to* be, she meant that other, civilised time before the dictatorship, before the war. I realised that for me the two *used to's* had merged into one.

Here and there, at the gates to the overgrown gardens where the grass grew as tall as a child, an old man stood, cap in hand, and cried as we passed.

'Je perçus des Funérailles, dans mon Cerveau' – these words came into my mind, and the priest's Orthodox chant and the rattle of his censer supplied the accompaniment:

> *Je perçus des Funérailles, dans mon Cerveau,*
> *Un Convoi allait et venait,*
> *Il marchait – marchait sans fin – je crus*
> *Que le Sens faisait irruption –*

I kept pace with Mamargot, who was herself again, first angry and then amused that Sabin had brought four men with hunting rifles to fire gun salutes at the grave.

'That's him all over,' she said quietly.

'So much is still to be achieved in this town for you good people,' Sabin said. He was dressed all in black and carried a black Astrakhan cap in his hand. Who wore old commie caps like that these days? Surely not even Sabin. And yet the way he acted, you'd have thought he'd doffed it only a moment before, out of respect for the deceased.

His presence wearied me. The four men with him were Austrians from Schweighofer Timber Company, friends of his son who had been forced to interrupt their logging work in the Carpathians while they waited for a corruption case to be settled. In the meantime, Sabin had wangled them hunting licences. They had, it seemed, shot a large bear the night before.

'Big-big! Huge!' one of them boasted, raising his hands, rifle and all, high above everyone's heads. But Sabin waved this aside and told us they'd only caught the bear after Ata had lured it with food – like back in the day with Ceaușescu. Austrians didn't know the first thing about hunting.

'Shhh,' one of the mourners said. 'Leave the dead to the dead and the living to the living.'

'But it's true,' Sabin said, encouraged. 'They're a puny bunch and haven't a clue how to hunt. I've seen some things, I can tell you ...'

'Plenty to see these days,' Yunus said, pulling Sabin away from us, towards the front of the procession.

Sabin clapped him on the shoulder. 'You wouldn't believe it,' he said. And half turning to us, he told us in a loud voice that the Austrians were such bad shots they'd had to chase the bear halfway across the mountain and ended up having to fish it out of the river.

'And now for the best bit,' he said, waiting for Margot and me to catch him up. 'Listen to this!' Because he'd charged the Austrians by weight for what they shot, the stingy bastards had been up all night drying the poor creature with a hair dryer. 'So it would weigh less!'

The power had cut four times in the Evening Star Guesthouse because of that hair dryer. 'Vrrr-vrrr! Wham! No power! Vrrr-Vrrr! Wham! No power again! Four times! After that the hair dryer packed up completely.'

He laughed and the men laughed with him.

'You'd better do a proper job of the gun salutes,' he warned them cheerfully. 'Nice and high, eh? Wouldn't want you hitting any of us.'

'No way,' Yunus said, amused.

At the cemetery the coffin was unloaded from the hearse, and two men carried it the rest of the way, because there was so little space between the graves.

Outside the vault, the priest poured red wine and oil over the white cloth in the form of a cross and said the beautiful prayer of King David: 'Purge me with hyssop, and I shall be clean: wash me, and I shall be whiter than snow.'

Then the coffin was closed, and the two men slung ropes around it, while the small gypsy climbed down with a bucket of mortar.

I can remember a lot of details from that day, but maybe I've mixed them up with subsequent media reports; looking back now, my own experiences seem unreal. I've had to struggle with my conscience. Is my resolve to stick to the truth even tenable, when my memories are so fragmented?

I feel great fatigue at the thought that I must prove myself credible, that my story must compete with all those strident media voices that are so much louder, so much more insistent. Proceeding from the assumption that you would read this report out of sheer sensationalism, I was tempted to start straight in on the gory events, the dead bodies, the faces frozen in horror, the impalings, the gouged-out eyes.

But that very assumption – that I would be read by the wrong person – stopped me in my tracks again. Why would I feed your lust for sensation?

Am I fishing for sympathy?

What's clear is that I must write down what happened, if only for myself, into the void, in the silent hope that there are readers out there who will understand my warning.

As I write this, I recall the tattoo that the small gypsy had on his right hand, between his thumb and index finger: a green quincunx, like the five pips on a die. He said it was prison code for *alone within four walls*.

Had he given himself the tattoo to remember his suffering, or in the hope that it would be seen and understood? Judging from the visible position of the quincunx, it seems safe to assume the latter – humans are communicative beings, though they may not always know with whom they are communicating.

I remember that as soon as the small gypsy was down in the vault, he began to scream shrilly. At first I thought it was Miss Sanda, but she was standing by the wreaths, smoothing out the bows. She was sulking and pretended not to hear the scream; the priest had been sharp with her a moment before, telling her to trust in faith, not superstition.

It had started when Margot tried to lay a bunch of flowers on the coffin. Miss Sanda had said it was unlucky to put them directly on the coffin: the deceased would sit up and bang her head on the lid and then notice she was dead – and other such nonsense.

'Faith, not superstition,' the usually docile priest had shouted. 'Faith, not superstition' – and he'd waved his arms around so wildly that the censer flew out on its long chains and hit one of the Austrians on the leg.

I can't remember whether the gun salutes were ever fired.

Someone handed me the small sack of exhumed bones to put back in the grave at the head of the coffin, and I took it, muttering to myself, 'At the head, at the head.' Then the shrill scream started up which I couldn't immediately locate.

I see myself, as in a dream, climbing down the ladder, my left arm twisted behind me to grasp the rungs. I saw women's legs in black silk stockings, heaps of flowers, the afflicted Austrian hopping on one leg. Then it grew darker. Flies buzzed fretfully and the stench was so intense that it robbed me of my presence.

Was there really green smoke down there (on which, more later)?

When I came to, I was standing in the vault, excited and dazed, my eyes watering. The scene before me gleamed indistinctly in the light of an upset lamp, and I remember the open niche on the left, and very nearby, on the right, the other wall of niches, where for some reason I expected to see a mirror. Further back, I thought I saw the small gypsy on the ground, and I headed towards him, the growing number of flies buzzing louder and louder in my ears.

He was lying on the stone engraved with the mating dogs, but when I touched him and he spun round, something trickled over my hand and flies swarmed out of empty eye sockets into my face.

A stream of dark blood came from his mouth, and his torn lips were pursed as if for a kiss.

I remember hurrying back up the ladder and saying the words that would later be quoted all over the media: 'There's somebody there.'

VIII

The Impaled Traian Fifor

THE POLICE AND TV CREW arrived at the same time; they seemed to know each other from previous operations.

'Evening, all,' the chief of police called from outside the vault. 'I've got a nice surprise for you.'

And he produced a roll of yellow barrier tape printed with the words *Crime Scene*.

Reporters and camera crew cheered.

They unpacked cameras, microphones and cables, and began to film under glaring illumination. This light, against the backdrop of the ruddy dusk, made for an atmosphere of storm, and there was a restlessness, as before a storm, among the people in the cemetery. Old peasants appeared here and there to light candles and weed their overgrown family plots. They worked hastily and with spirit, constantly peering over at our vault; when interviewed that evening, they said we'd been known in B. for years, though only vaguely, and had a bit of a reputation as snobs, always looking down on others – God only knew what we were capable of.

It didn't occur to any of *us* to talk to the media. What would we have said? That we knew nothing about the dead man? None of the journalists sought us out either; there were enough random bystanders jostling to be heard, eager to broadcast their ignorance and their fear. Only the chief of police asked us, very politely, a few routine questions and gave us permission to wall in Madame Didina's coffin the next day. He said the dead man was probably a tramp done in by another tramp, under the influence. Nothing out of the ordinary – we had no cause for concern. Geo shook his hand several times when we left.

Our friends from Bucharest stayed on for a few days, and some of them longer, to be there for us through what followed. Good hosts that we were, we found that a lot of our conversations revolved around their news. They told us about their children and grandchildren who were living picture-perfect lives in London, Zurich and Boston, and they produced photos and newspaper clippings and company brochures in evidence. The mood was cheerful and our friends lively as they got up to fetch things and passed round photos and gravy boats, touching each other or even hugging as they spoke. But I think I sensed a numb sadness in us even so – at being in the wrong place, on the wrong side of life.

'We were all set to sell up,' Madame Tudoran told us. 'Our country house in Sinaia, the vineyards in Mitrofani – even our Bucharest house near Cișmigiu Park. We were going to sell the lot – everything we own – and buy ourselves a nice chic little apartment in Zurich, close to the kids. Something small by the lake or on the hill behind the opera house – something we could leave to the children. But there was nothing, can you believe it. All we'd have got for our money was a tiny flat in a working-class area. 1960s architecture. I can't tell you how awful it was. A dingy place with nylon carpet, over-looking a dank courtyard.'

We all burst out laughing – not least because Mamargot said dramatically, 'Quelle horreur!'

And as we got up from table, talk turned instead to what we would eat at the next meal, and the guests quar-relled enthusiastically over which of them was to cook.

Yunus was among those who cooked for us; he made Middle Eastern food with ingredients bought specially in Brașov. There was spicy lentil soup with flat bread, falafel with humous and tahini, tabbouleh with masses of parsley and lemon, a dip made with za'atar, another dip – muhammara – made with red peppers and walnuts, a big bowl of that refreshing minty yoghurt dish called labneh, and baba ghanoush, which is an aubergine dip like ours, but with tahini and garlic and topped with pomegranate seeds. To finish off there was cardamom mocha with ma'amoul, a kind of semolina biscuit filled with nuts, and – thrill of thrills – a gurgling narghile from Brașov for the smokers among us, or anyone who just wanted a go at the fruity water pipe.

I couldn't eat a thing, but everyone was so busy helping themselves to mezze that nobody noticed. I'd barely eaten for days and yet I wasn't hungry. What did it mean? I had the impression that nothing on the table was edible; the soft, mushy consistency of what the others were eating hardly seemed a compelling reason to eat with them – indeed, the cheerful gathering was suddenly as unreal to me as a troupe of shadow puppets.

The guests exhaled white smoke whose shadows coiled up the walls as if pulled on grey strings. The room filled with a sickly-sweet apple smell, and Yunus was much complimented on his cooking – with a feast like that you didn't even notice the lack of meat.

'Better without meat,' I said, as I used to say as a child.

And our friends began to reminisce about the past, when Bucharest was full of Arab students, especially medics. Ceaușescu had been careful to keep in with the Arab dictatorships because he needed oil and had plans to invest in petrochemicals. Yunus said that at least four of his relatives had studied in Romania; they all had wonderful memories of the country, and now he did too. He was keen to stay.

'A true patriot,' Geo said and repeated the anecdote about Yunus mistaking 'Gaudeamus Igitur' for the Romanian national anthem.

Everyone laughed loudly, and then they raised their glasses and sang:

> *Gaudeamus igitur,*
> *Iuvenes dum sumus!*
> *Post iucundam iuventutem,*
> *Post molestam senectutem,*
> *Nos habebit humus.*

Later in the meal – which I sat through, as I say, with a complete lack of appetite, though not without an initial show of interest in the conversation of those I called friends – I came up with a novel way of entertaining myself. It is important that I mention this to you here because, as I gradually came to realise, the form this entertainment took was revelatory of my altered state.

It began with a sigh.

It was a long, but relatively quiet sigh, and I was astonished to see the unfortunate effect it had on the gestures and postures of the guests, who immediately slumped on the table like discarded marionettes. I hastily breathed in again, and lo and behold, the scene was pulled straight, and everyone talked and gesticulated as before.

I couldn't believe my eyes. I sighed once more and the same thing happened: everyone collapsed in a heap. What was going on? I began to take long, slow breaths, watching closely to see what would happen next – and when I held my breath, everyone froze. I padded round the table, fetched the water pipe from bearded Mr Tudoran and sat back down with it; as I sucked on it and it began to bubble, I noticed that the guests were waving their arms about. *Blub–blub–blub* went the water in the green glass bowl. *Blub–blub*. And the guests' arms waved and waved.

I puffed out a cloud of white smoke, and a loud roar made all the flowers in the vases shed their petals. Was I dreaming? I breathed more and more quickly, fast-forwarding events towards their end with jerky, agitated movements, while the accompanying soundtrack played in my ears, high and mocking.

As I write this, a memory of my childhood friend Arina forces itself upon me. We are sitting in the garden, disinclined to move. In front of us, on a big stone, is the blue dust of a lapis lazuli which we have gone to great lengths to grind into Fra Angelico blue for a picture we are going to paint together. Then a breeze gets up and the fine powder is gone.

Miss Sanda took her bucket and cloths to the cemetery and hung around by the yellow barrier tape, waiting to be let through to the vault.

'My trusty one,' Margot said to her. 'You work too hard. Why don't you go and have a rest?'

The dead man, Miss Sanda told us, had yet to be identified; he was in too much of a mess. His eyes had been poked out, probably with a fork, and pieces of his tongue had been cut off. Also, his belly had been speared through with a sharp instrument, narrowly missing his liver and kidneys; the poor man had probably bled to death – a very slow death, people said. No blood had been found in the vault, though, so he must have been killed elsewhere and moved there later. But why? Who would want to threaten us?

'Oh, my trusty one,' Margot said, 'don't think about these things. Go and have a rest.'

Margot was forever telling Miss Sanda to rest or take it easy, and I would even venture to say that it wouldn't have bothered her in the least if the indefatigable Sanda had simply stopped working for us one fine day and taken to lounging around on one of the ottomans or garden benches – indeed, it's quite possible that Mamargot wouldn't even have noticed her absence, for she was invariably surrounded by exuberant guests keen to help out in the garden or kitchen.

'Just go and have a rest,' she said to Miss Sanda, but it wasn't in Miss Sanda's nature to rest – not because of any sense of duty towards us, but because she was unaware of even the possibility of idleness. That, at least, was my impression at the time.

When we went for a walk and Miss Sanda accompanied us for a stretch – on her way to the cemetery again, to make sure that all was *in order* – she never looked about her, but only stared at the asphalt, and when we stopped en route to look at one of the grand old villas or admire a bird in the sweeping fir branches overhead, she would impatiently jangle the handle of her bucket, or nudge something away with her foot – a dried plant or a toad squashed flat by a car. Then came the incident with the journalist who accosted Sabin in the cemetery. Dead people voted in B., he yelled; there were dead people on the electoral lists; everyone knew that Sabin and his son rigged the elections. While the rest of us were still digesting this information, Miss Sanda scuttled off with her bucket and cloths, determined not to miss the fight.

That evening she brought us news of the body in our vault, giving us as all the details she could remember. The eyes hadn't been poked out with a fork after all, but more likely pecked out by birds; the holes in the tongue also appeared to be the work of beaks. This meant that the man must have died with his tongue sticking out, though it wasn't yet clear why. What was clear was the body's identity: it was a man who'd emigrated to Spain more than ten years previously – Traian Fifor, forty years old.

Back in the day, Miss Sanda said, she'd worked with his mother in the weaving mill; his father had been fired for telling jokes about the Communists – and for making an illegal schnapps machine out of stolen piping. Traian had been quite a card, like his father – we might remember. But he'd got married, believe it or not – 'to a whore,' Miss Sanda said; it seemed the woman had found work in Spain, and Traian had followed her there. Like everyone else, they'd returned to B. every summer to work on the house they were building. They must have separated, though, because after two or three summers the building work had been abandoned.

Traian's parents were dead; his brothers and sisters had emigrated like him, but no one knew what had become of them. About a year ago Traian had been the object of some scam in Spain, making him a source of considerable amusement to the people of B. But no one could say when he'd come back; apparently he'd lived in his parents' house without the neighbours noticing. Apparently the place stank to high heavens.

'God forgive him,' said Margot, and the others echoed her.

'Poor guy,' Geo said, 'goes away to make his fortune and then comes back and meets with this awful death.'

Geo's words left us all quite moved, so I kept quiet and didn't mention that I had known Traian Fifor very well.

In any case, I wanted to see a photo of him before I said anything, just to be sure.

And for the first time here in B., I wished I had internet.

The only internet access was up a hill on the road to Brașov. Our friends, and especially Geo, drove there regularly, but I'd never been.

Maybe I should explain something to you. I had returned to this remote village to see Margot, and to think and paint in peace. What I wanted, for me and for my art, was to rediscover the old primacy of the senses and re-establish direct contact with nature – to rub up against the material world in my day-to-day life in a way that can only be done in a simple, primitive place. The once current idea that the internet would democratise education, spread knowledge and reinforce moral values had been reduced to ruins – why be distracted by those ruins as long as we had this little piece of nature here in secluded B.?

As I walked up the hill, internetwards, I found myself alongside an old peasant couple and asked them the way.

'Internet Hill?' they said. 'Just keep on up.'

They too were heading that way, to skype with their grown-up children in Italy.

And so I walked with them.

It was sunny today, they said, like in Sicily, where their children lived. In Sicily you could go to the beach every day and swim for hours. The sand there was very fine; their kids were really happy.

The two of them were breathing heavily, partly because of the steep climb and partly because they were so anxious to tell me everything – about the wonderful lives their kids and little grandkids were leading, about the pay rises, the outstanding school reports, the sports prizes, the capaciousness of the family car, the big lump of savings in the bank.

'Great,' I said. 'Excellent.' And: 'Bravo, you must be proud.'

'Oh, we are,' they said, and there was no mistaking the mocking tone in their voices.

So what did I do, they asked.

'I'm on holiday,' I said.

They laughed, not without scorn. They knew that, they said; I was Mrs Margot's daughter (I nodded and let that pass). But what did I do in life, what was my job?

'I paint pictures,' I said. 'I'm an artist.'

'An artist?' they asked with one voice, and the man added, 'How much do you earn with that?'

'Loads,' I said, and the rest of the walk passed in silence.

At the top of the hill, dozens of people were shouting at their phones, and children and grandchildren were answering on the screens.

'Is Matteo top of the class again?'

'What did you get him? A bike?'

I sat as far away from them as I could to read the papers, using the little tablet I'd bought in a Paris junkshop. I found what I was looking for in the 'Most viewed' section of the *adevarul.ro* news site: *Impaled in Transylvania: A mysterious death makes world news.*

A small photograph showed the skewered Traian Fifor in the vault. To the right of the pixelated image was a portrait photo of him, alive, in his military uniform. I immediately recognised those big eyes of his, staring out at me in bewilderment, as if he'd foreseen his hideous end.

A sudden howl at my side made me jump. 'You're Grandma's precious, Chiara, you do know that, don't you? Tell me you do.' I tactfully moved away from the old woman, who proceeded to exclaim between sobs, 'All right, amore, all right, I'll stop crying now, I promise.'

The trouble was that as soon as you escaped the throng of people yelling at their phones, the internet reception cut out. I settled down without Wi-Fi to stare at Traian's photo.

I was quite a young girl when I first fell in love with him. I used to watch him go barefoot to fetch the cow from the paddock in the evenings, his arms draped over a long hazel switch at his neck, his hands dangling casually, his chest swollen with pride – more James Dean than yoked peasant. He could whistle loudly. He whistled to the cow and to the horses in the paddock; he whistled the geese off the road. He whistled animals over or whistled them away again, and there was often something slightly teasing in that whistle of his.

'Hi-da-day,' he would call, on the few occasions when he wasn't whistling – and it sounded surprised and amused, as if he were saying: *Seriously, now, guys*, though without quite taking himself seriously.

Once he jumped out of a tree onto the back of a grazing carthorse. The terrified creature galloped off down the paddock with him and tore through the forest and over the river at breakneck speed. Traian clung on with arms and legs, and let the horse have its way. It wasn't until they reached the next village that he summoned the courage to jump off – outside the Evening Star, of all places, a hotel patronised by Communist big shots and their wives.

Afterwards, Traian never missed an opportunity to mimic the astonished big shots and their dolled-up wives startled by his demon ride, and he would invariably finish the performance by pulling up his threadbare shirt to show us the welts from the whipping his father had given him. He claimed not to have felt the lashes: what didn't kill him, he said, only made him stronger.

I can see him now, sitting on the white milestone at the bend in the road, a blade of grass in his mouth. I see the grass twitch upwards for a second as the corners of his mouth move in greeting.

'What are you doing there?' I asked.

'Waiting for something to happen,' he said.

'What?'

'Don't know,' he said, bursting into that cheerful laugh of his. I laughed too. And then he explained to me how spiders fly.

We kissed sitting on a big tree stump by the field where there would one day be an old Dacia with cold drinks and pretzels for sale. Traian had bad tooth decay and his front teeth were riddled with little holes like shot holes, but it didn't bother me. True love, I knew, required an effort of will.

I held out my phone towards the signal to read about Traian's death. On the blueish screens of the assembled inhabitants of B., children's faces flickered, and here and there I spotted the pixelated image of Traian's body and the portrait photo of him in military uniform. Close beside me an old man was watching a football video; I don't know why the memory is so vivid. A drumming sound came from his phone and vigorous shouts of 'Olé, olé, olé, oléééé ...'

I entered *Traian Fifor* into the search engine and was amazed at how many hits he had. His picture and the news of his impalement were to be found on *theguardian*, *rfi*, *spiegel*, *nytimes* and *oglobo*, as well as a number of blogs, and there were tweets under *#traianfifor*, *#impaler*, *#draculaproof*, *#translyvania* and *#țeapă*.

The longest article was on *adevarul.ro*. Citing international media reports which in turn cited reports from the local press, it informed its readers that the mutilated corpse of a certain Traian Fifor had been discovered by funeral mourners in their family vault, and that the corpse showed clear signs of impalement as practised in the mid-fifteenth century at the time of Count Vlad the Impaler.

In those days, it seemed, a condemned man was laid on the ground, arms and legs tightly bound, and henchmen would drive a greased, sharpened stake into his anus, carefully past his kidneys and heart, and out through his mouth or neck – the side of his neck, that is, between head and shoulder. This done, the stake would be driven into the ground, and the impaled man, thus displayed as a deterrent, would slither a little way down the stake and die slowly and pitifully of indescribable pain and thirst, further tortured by ravens swarming down on him to peck out his eyes and tongue, and tear his flesh from his body.

By this method, enemy Turks – their turbans still on their heads – had been impaled by Prince Vlad in the mid-fifteenth century; but murderers, thieves and corrupt Boyars had likewise met this gruesome end.

Drac's Back, *The Sun* titled, and *La Libération* confirmed: *L'Empaleur de retour en Transylvanie*. The final paragraph of the *adevarul* article explained that Prince Vlad the Impaler had, if not in his lifetime, then later in the history books, been hailed as a harsh but fair father and remained a popular figure in Romania to this day. The lines addressed to him by national poet Mihai Eminescu in 1881, at a time of rampant political corruption, were finding increasing resonance in the country:

> *Impaler, lord, wouldst thou but come*
> *To rule with iron fist.*

Because of the semantic shift of the verb 'to be impaled', which in modern-day usage suggests self-inflicted failure – a Romanian will yell, 'Țeapă!' (literally, 'Stake!') as an English speaker might say, 'Fail!' – the other articles recommended to me by the algorithm were all about more figurative forms of impalement: *Ţeapă! Romanian Waiter Impaled in Spain – customers conga their way out of the bar without paying.*

Ţeapă idiotă! Romanian Thieves Impale Themselves in Sicily – bakery burglars try to steal the till and take the scales instead!

Impaled on the Op Table – these celebs got facelifts from a bouncer!

Pension Rise – Ţeapă colosală! New government drives a thick stake through voters' hearts.

When I looked up from the screen, a stabbing pain pierced my head, powerful as a blow. I walked home in a daze, my back hunched, all kinds of nonsense running through my mind – ridiculous stuff about the heat of the desert dealing Lawrence of Arabia a blow to the head like a sword. Just like a sword! I hurried home.

In my room I drew the curtains and went to bed in broad daylight. I fell into a restless sleep.

When I woke it was dark. I sat up in bed slowly, as if pulled by a big metal spring. My body, I noticed, was as tense as that of a young animal catching its first scent.

The night was fresh; pale moonlight came in through a chink in the curtains. Somewhere in the house I could hear a low breathing and sighing and the occasional rustle of sheets – sounds that held the space around me stretched taut.

My instinct, though, was to go out, onto the balcony, and so I followed my shadow through the rooms, gliding silently over the usually creaky parquet. Only the curtains shifted slightly as I stepped out through the narrow crack between them.

I felt the cool of the countryside on my face. The forest lay bright and still – almost, I thought, as if turned to stone. I'd never seen it like that before; it made it easy for me to spot things moving – creatures of the night, most of them unsuspecting.

IX

The Prince's Grave

THE NEXT MORNING, Mamargot woke me; it was Sunday, and divine liturgy in B. for once. Since there were so many of us, the priest from the neighbouring parish had agreed to hold mass in our church.

Mamargot set down a tray of breakfast on my bed; there was more food, she said, in the drawing room.

'A feast!' I cried, though I wasn't hungry.

Outside, a storm was brewing with that suddenness that you only get in the mountains. The light shimmered like metal under low grey clouds. Mamargot loved stormy weather, and so, to make her happy, I looked up from the coffee I was cradling in my hands and told her how much I loved weather like this.

'So do I!' Mamargot said. 'I've loved it ever since I was a child.'

Just before mass, it began to pour. Outside the open church door, the water fell like an endless curtain while we stood closely packed in the nave, shrouded in a veil of brightness. The steam from our clothes and the smoke from the incense broke the light, making us look illuminated.

As jingling bells announced the advance of the priest's swinging censer, people ducked out of the way, and whenever we made the sign of the cross, we bumped elbows with the people next to us and felt arms knock into our backs as those behind us also crossed themselves.

Then the priest called out, 'The doors! The doors! Let us attend in wisdom!' And we raised our voices in the creed, speaking it good and loud so as to be heard above the drone of the rain. Mamargot and I were at the very front on the left, and when I glanced up, I saw us reflected in the glass of the icon of the Virgin in front of us. At first I thought we were part of the icon.

I remember the sermon well; unlike others, it has stuck in my head. The priest switched on the chandelier – a dim light filled the church – and he turned to us and said, 'God has delivered every one of us, even those whose dwelling places are full of the filth and rot of this world. He has delivered us, as he delivered the possessed Gadarene who dwelt among the tombs.' At this mention of the possessed man, the priest looked at Mamargot and me, so that everyone else turned to look at us too. Those words, he said, were from Nicolae Steinhardt. Mamargot and I nodded knowingly.

It was a sermon, then, about the man possessed by demons who jumped out from the tombs and frightened people. Asked by Christ what he was called, the man replied, 'My name is Legion: for we are many.'

A truly strange business, the priest said, for there is no such thing as an anonymous, impersonal existence – there is no existence without personal responsibility. Everyone has a name, even the angels. Even the fallen angels. But the demons in this man sought safety in numbers and called themselves Legion.

'Legion,' the priest intoned loudly, gazing around the church. To my left Miss Sanda sat with lowered head, quietly drooling onto her chest.

The demons recognised Christ's power and complained that he had come to torment them before the time, which is to say before the Last Judgment. They insisted on their right to be free until then, for that right – the right to free choice – had been given by God to everyone: Adam and Eve, and even the fallen angels. But Christ ordered the demons to come out of the man, for with their freedom they were robbing another of *his* freedom, the possessed man, who was no longer master of himself.

'Do you understand?' the priest asked, and he paused. The storm swelled louder in the silence, then gave way to the swish of cloth against cloth as people shifted in their seats; some crossed themselves in the commotion.

Knowing that Christ would refuse to let them enter other humans, the devils asked his permission to enter some pigs instead. And Christ agreed. Whereupon the devils entered the pigs and immediately hurled themselves off a cliff into the sea.

'Their aim, you see, was to plunge to the depths and bring others to ruin along the way.'

Here the priest warned of anonymous persons and apparitions who come to us in the name of an alleged right or truth, promising great things if we let them in – such promises, he said, could only end in our fall.

'Do not let them in, for without your consent they have no power over you!'

Might 'great and rich mercies' be bestowed upon us, the priest said, raising his arms, and the next thing we knew, Mayor Sabin was striding to the front of the church, flourishing a large piece of paper and asking permission to announce something important, some good news.

Permission was granted.

Sabin cleared his throat ostentatiously and waited for silence. Then he launched into a rambling, self-adulatory speech, taking his time to get to the shocking news.

'Dear citizens!' he began.

We had been through some tough days, he said unctuously – eventful days. He, in particular, with his mayoral responsibilities, had had a great deal to do and a great deal to take care of, and this was now a good time and place for him to ask all those of us whose noses he might have put out of joint, whether intentionally or unintentionally – especially unintentionally, he said with a wink. So, what he wanted was to ask us, in all humility, as was appropriate to this house of God – in all humility and without beating about the bush – we knew him, always short and to the point. He wanted to ask us – to forgive him.

The congregation began to mutter.

'Where would we be otherwise?' Sabin asked. He laughed engagingly, and a number of peasants laughed with him.

The ghastly discovery, he continued, in the vault of a venerable Bucharest family – and here he bowed so slowly to Mamargot that everyone around us turned to look at her again. A venerable family, he went on, who, God knows, had already endured trials enough – yes, this ghastly discovery had brought to light something unexpected, but if you asked him, he would say, in all humility and – yes, why not? – with a degree of pride, that it had happened at a very opportune time, because this was the year when our country was celebrating the centenary of the unification of Greater Romania.

Someone began to clap, others shushed them and Sabin said with gusto that this was fantastic news coming after such difficult days, and if he were in a less hallowed place he would say (and here he lowered his voice to a stage whisper) that every kick in the arse was a great step for mankind. General hilarity ensued.

Then Sabin paused to confer softly with the priest, and, as I'm sure you can imagine, people began to grow restless again and several journalists called out, 'What did they find, Mr Mayor? Tell us.'

At length Sabin turned back to the congregation and asked us, please, to permit him to read the announcement from his notes – he was very moved by it, as no doubt we all would be, and he didn't want to leave anything out in the excitement.

He began to read. It was a long-winded text about the history of B., a muddled chronicle full of dates from the

Middle Ages when the huge Janissary armies of the Ottomans were defeated here by Romanian princes who, unlike their opponents, had only a handful of plucky soldiers at their command, but were nevertheless cunning enough to burn the fields and poison the wells on the campaign route of the Ottoman army, and not to leave any animals behind, but to hide them all in the mountains, from where they launched surprise attacks on their demoralised opponents.

'Did you get this out of a textbook?' a journalist yelled, provoking general amusement, but also calls for more respect.

But Sabin held up a finger and said he only wanted to remind us who we were – namely, no more nor less than Europe's saviours, for if our ancestors hadn't fought off the pagans here at the gates of civilisation, martyring themselves in battle after battle, the rest of Europe would never have been able to build their vast cathedrals.

The church began to empty.

Sabin raised his voice. He would keep it brief, he said. Here, in the cemetery of B., in the vault of a venerable Bucharest family, an unfortunate man had been found murdered. We all knew about it; some of us were here in B. to report on it. As usual in such a case, the crime scene had been searched and – more bodies had been found.

I didn't get the joke until I heard everyone around me laughing.

'Seriously, though, now,' Sabin said. They had, he said, examined the place where the corpse had been discovered, and it turned out that the old gravestone where the body had been found was of priceless value.

At this point he held up a piece of paper. It showed a picture of the gravestone with the mating dogs.

'Look at this, dear Romanians,' he said with great pathos, holding the paper up to the church chandelier. 'Look what we found.'

I don't know whether it was the strain of holding the picture up for so long or the emotion it evoked, but his hands began to tremble and his eyes watered in the gleam of the chandelier.

He had, he said, consulted specialists from the Museum of History in Bucharest, eminent professors who had confirmed what he'd suspected – and what any journalist worth his salt must surely have noticed too. Didn't we recognise this battle here? Had we forgotten our country's glorious past?

People began to mutter again; everyone spoke at once.

On this great day, Sabin concluded solemnly, on this glorious day when a chapter of our history had been brought alive to us – the heroic deeds, no less, of our illustrious forefathers – on this day, he had been hoping, in his capacity as mayor, to invite us to raise a glass with him in celebration out in the churchyard, only sadly it seemed to be raining – but the drinks had merely been postponed and would be all the more lavish when the time came.

'What's with the gravestone?' I called out, prompted by Mamargot.

Sabin smiled gratefully at me. Then, loudly and with great pomp, he explained that the grave discovered in our vault could be that of only one man – a man who had fought here and defeated many enemies, only to be deceitfully murdered, killed like a martyr. He was talking, of course, of the valiant prince of world fame – our very own Prince Vlad the Impaler.

A whoop went up from the congregation, and the priest said solemnly, 'Amen!'

As you can imagine, the news caught us off our guard. What do you do when your family vault turns out to be harbouring the grave of a famous prince – *the* famous Romanian prince – especially when the news comes smack in the year of Romania's centenary, just as politicians all over the country are eagerly resurrecting national heroes of every ilk, the more ancient the better, to distract from their endless corruption and mismanagement?

The surprise nature of the news and the failure to inform us of the discovery on our property before announcing it to the public reminded Mamargot of the Communist expropriation of our villa. She was so angry that a blood vessel burst in her eye – a painful sight, the pupil surrounded by dark-red blood – and for the rest of that Sunday she could talk of only two things: the pack of rubbernecks and so-called patriots who would soon be trooping in and out of the vault like visitors to Lenin's mausoleum – and her sunglasses which she had mislaid somewhere in the house just when she could have done with them.

'How are we related to the prince?' Geo asked, struggling to contain his unwelcome enthusiasm.

But who could say? Who knew anything about our genealogy?

The topic depressed Margot – soon they'd all be storming in on us; someone might have warned her.

Then, at dinner, Geo launched into a rant about all Romanians having the right to know their history. People didn't even know the history of their own families, he complained – their parents had told them nothing in that infamous era; the Communist dictatorship had drained dry the river of knowledge and rewritten schoolbooks in line with state doctrine . . .

'It's true,' Ninel said. 'I'm afraid Geo's right.'

Geo said solemnly that we must re-establish our ties with the past, because until we knew where we came from, we would never know who we were – or who we ought to be. Now it emerged that we were descended from the most illustrious prince of the Romanian land. That's right, Geo said with spirit, the coat of arms on the tombstone – the triumphant dragon, symbol of Christianity – could be that of only one man: the fearless prince without whom, as the philosopher Emil Cioran had once said, our country's history would be nothing but a big field of sheep. For Prince Vlad alone had marked our history, punctured it – impaled it, no less – with firm resolve. Before and after him – to this day, alas – Romania's history was no more than a desolate waste of stupidity and herd mentality.

'Quelle horreur!' Mamargot cried, covering her bloody eye with her hand.

The next day I drove her to Brașov where we bought ourselves big sunglasses and engaged four security guards from an agency to protect the family vault. These guards were massively built men with a stern gaze, and we were assured they were incorruptible – 'of sound Transylvanian morals, positively German.'

X

Dracula's Entry into B.

I TRIED TO RECALL WHAT TRAIAN's mutilated corpse had looked like – I regretted not having examined it for longer. All I remembered were the gouged-out eyes buzzing with flies, and the mouth spewing dark blood over my wrists. If only I'd looked more closely.

'Sure you're brave enough to walk hand in hand with me?' Traian had asked me all those years ago by the big tree stump.

'Of course,' I'd said, taking his hand.

He hadn't expected that and looked about him, startled.

We walked into the forest without a word.

It was perhaps afternoon, the forest bathed in a quivering light – I remember the smell of rotten wood and steam rising from the leaves. We walked quickly but aimlessly, down hills and then up again, tripping over bulging roots so that we could grip each other's hands even tighter and tell each other, 'Careful!' When

I stooped to pick wild strawberries, I pulled him down with me. *Your hand in mine is like a part of me.* Who said that again? Our hands were sweaty, our fingers interlocked, this clasp the firmest part of our two bodies.

Eventually we came to the river whose waters had risen, making it roil and froth in places.

'Come on,' Traian said, 'let's cross over to the hazels.'

We tramped into the water. I walked upstream from Traian, holding his hand tight.

Part way across he tripped over a rock, teetered and lost my hand. I made a lunge for him and caught him.

'Don't be scared,' he said, laughing. 'Don't be scared, I'm here.'

Once on the other shore I teased him: *he* was the one who should have been scared, not me; I could swim.

'No one can swim in this river,' he said.

'Yes, they can.'

'No way.'

'Want to bet?'

We kissed on the mouth.

He had little black holes in his front teeth, but it didn't bother me. And because it didn't bother me, I thought it was love.

A vague premonition drew me out of bed. It was night. I crossed the parquet without a sound, my white nightdress trailing on the floor. I opened the French windows to the balcony, passed the moon reflected in the glass, heard a sigh that might have been my own.

He was standing at the stone balustrade with his back to me.

'Here I am,' I said and held out my arms to him.

Can you follow me? Are you brave enough? I was in the process, you see, of turning away from what I had hitherto called my life.

Day was breaking, however, with a dazzling light that cut hard edges into the shadows, separating the pale from the dark. Over everything hung the smell of grilled meatballs – a smell that thoroughly disgusted me and to which I responded with my habitual lack of appetite.

Do you know James Ensor's painting, *Christ's Entry into Brussels in 1889*? Christ himself is barely visible, but the ugly masses celebrating him – and, in effect, themselves – are very much in evidence, overpoweringly so.

A similar sight was to be seen at the carnival in B. soon after Sabin announced the discovery of Prince Vlad's grave. Everyone was appalled by the shocking news, but no one wanted to miss out on a visit to somewhere so talked about.

'I have resuscitated B.!' Sabin boasted.

When I went down in my dark glasses he was sitting on one of the benches under the lilacs, a little coffee cup in his hand which he held by its short handle between finger and thumb, his other fingers splayed.

Now that there were so many people in B. again, he said, he wanted to ask us fine people for our support. Nothing that would put us to any trouble or inconvenience – just an extra dose of trust in the man who'd been taking care of the place for the past forty years. This wasn't the time to argue over details; it was the moment to act – to get things done. It was now or never!

He came straight to the point. The hordes were here – B. had never been so full. Margot had to open her vault to visitors. She just had to. It was no big deal.

But Margot, her eyes, like mine, concealed behind a large pair of shades, repeated her polite refusal. She didn't want strangers in the family vault, she said, not for all the money in the world, and she was perfectly entitled to her decision.

They weren't strangers, Sabin insisted, and he was a pathetic sight: sweaty and red in the face, that strand of hair flopping over his forehead.

He glanced at me as if gauging my willingness to second him, but saw at once that I was no more enamoured of his business proposition than Margot. I, too, was made of granite.

We weren't talking passing trade, Sabin explained; the vault would be visited exclusively by eminent professors with a duty towards our nation's history and by leaders of our country who simply wished to light a candle to the souls of our ancestors. Of course, this being a democracy, there would also be some well-disposed journalists – friends of his – and sure, the odd tourist too, but these would be Romanian pilgrims, people of a contemplative bent, and of course a certain number of foreign travellers keen to get to grips with our history and traditions. We couldn't forbid these people access to the great Vlad the Impaler, prince of all Wallachians and forefather of all present-day Romanians!

'I'm not forbidding anything,' Margot said with exquisite politeness. 'I am simply insisting on my rights as an individual. I am sure you understand.'

'Of course,' I said, 'everyone understands. Have they found out who killed Traian Fifor yet?'

Sabin looked taken aback.

I repeated my question and Mamargot probed a little further. 'Did they ever get to the bottom of who killed that man and left him on our grave?'

'What do I know?' Sabin blurted out.

'Well, if you don't know, I don't know who would.' Margot said.

Sabin hesitated for a beat too long, then collected himself and laughed. 'You've got me there,' he said and let Margot fill his coffee cup.

She was right, he said: he'd had some pointers from the police station in Sinaia – they were getting on nicely with the case – but, as he was sure we understood, he was not in a position to pass anything on. One thing he could say, though, between ourselves, as old acquaintances – almost friends, in fact, so to speak. Such cases were the result of moral decay in Romania. He wasn't saying things had been better under Ceaușescu – God forbid. But there had been more law and order in those days. More patriotism. More respect in general for authority.

I admired Mamargot for the subtle gesture with which she signalled to Sabin that it was time for him to go, and then rose as he got to his feet and took her leave with a hint of regret at his departure.

Yes, Sabin said hastily, he had things to do as well. We'd made him forget the time; it was getting late. But he *would* just say before he left that Romania was going morally downhill fast – Margot must have noticed; she moved in fine circles – and it was precisely because of that moral decline that they were in such dire need of a historical role model like Vlad the Impaler. Margot really ought to reconsider this business with the vault – really – the sooner the better; he would strongly urge her to think again.

The descendants of heroes had a duty, did they not, to pass on their moral legacy to the nation's people – or at least not to withhold it from them. And now so many of the people of our nation had come here to B. He'd brought new life to B., and now new life – new moral standards – could pour out of B. into the rest of the country. Soon B. would be the centre of Romania – the centre of the whole world.

No sooner had he closed the gate behind him than Miss Sanda called out of the window, 'Can I beat the carpets now?'

'Yes, of course, my good woman,' Mamargot said. 'We're quite done here.'

I listened to the dull thuds of the carpet beater as if I were tracking the beats of my own heart. They sounded familiar.

Too soon, though, Mamargot called out to Miss Sanda, 'That'll do, my trusty one. You'll have us all choking if you don't stop!'

Immediately the vulgar sounds of Sabin's carnival assailed my ears again, making me witness to riotous events I would have preferred to ignore.

There was no looking away; Dracula's entry into B. thrust itself upon me, a picture I couldn't ignore. In the festive red, yellow and blue of the Romanian flag, with gusts of green blowing in from the Carpathians and a dab of white here and there, a crowd of people, masked and unmasked, made their way down the steep road. Officials and clergy, Sabin and Ata in ceremonial sashes, men in suits, the four Austrians with their rifles, old women in headscarves, wizened old men waving calloused hands at the cameras, hip young men with meticulously trimmed beards filming themselves on their phones, young women with pouting red lips taking selfies with the flags as backdrop, the occasional old peasant who had, of course, to strut past the assembled cameras of the world press with a rusty spade just as the news was starting – and, high above the crowd on a long pole, the wooden goat's head, decked out by the goat dancers with colourful bows and pompoms.

It wouldn't have been a proper carnival, of course, if there hadn't also been a fiddler, streams of bubbles, a few beggars, the old woman with magenta hair eating candy floss, big tasselled flags bearing the royal arms, strings of bunting, and masses of school children milling around in groups while their teachers gesticulated at the cameras.

A loudspeaker blared 'I've been looking for freedom', an injured child screamed without let-up and a man hammered away at the roof of a wooden souvenir kiosk.

Inside the kiosk, meanwhile, waiting to be bought, were the usual shepherd's pipes you couldn't get a sound out of, besoms, wicker baskets, handcrafted carpet beaters (yes, those too), bunting, plastic vuvuzelas and sundry kinds of jam.

So that was Sabin's festival in honour of Prince Vlad the Impaler!

In the days that followed, a handful of foreign tourists arrived with big rucksacks in B. When they asked for a campsite, Sabin must have told them that the bear had a habit of showing up at the river, and that they'd be better off camping in the gardens, preferably those of the abandoned houses. We later discovered that he'd pocketed a tidy fee for 'Campsite/High Season', and even had tickets printed with the triumphant dragon of the Ordo Draconis – the ornament and pride of the town.

And so here and there between the old houses and the tall unfinished buildings, brightly coloured tents began to sprout, washing lines went up, and in the evenings people sat around flickering bonfires, eating, drinking the local homemade Dracula schnapps, talking in loud voices – and quite often screaming, too, when the bats flew about.

The rest of the time, the tourists sauntered around on the lookout for vampires or a potential Dracula; they were curiously willing to find everything in B. bizarre, primitive and repellent. The few remaining peasants popped out of their houses as if on cue and walked around with grim-looking faces, living proof of their alleged otherness.

In the old phone box outside our house, a miniature library was set up, devoted exclusively to works about vampires.

Mamargot and Ninel rushed out for books to read in the garden, mainly because they wanted to get back to reading English.

I remember one novel in particular, from which Mamargot read whole passages out loud; perhaps it was the simplicity of it that charmed us. It was the story of a young woman and a handsome vampire, whose life together was one long, anguished abstinence.

Mamargot confessed that she didn't understand all the words, but she said it only made the book more entertaining.

XI

The Irrepressible Thirst for Death

SOME NIGHTS I FANCIED MYSELF back in the old B. of the past, where all was quiet and tranquil.

As I walked up the road, there was a strong smell of grass and earth and that resinous damp that made my breath quiver. I heard birds that I knew from childhood and felt they were calling to me not to forget. How long ago all that was. At some of the pale stones along the way I stopped to weep. After a while, though, I wept less, because I was stopping for the sole purpose of weeping – and eventually I stopped less too. I strode through the night with big springy steps, as if I knew where I was going.

Ah yes, with every night that passed, I felt a power, an obscure force, growing inside me, and when the white mist rose, I noticed that I was throwing my arms around like an army general urging his soldiers into battle. But what battle? And who was the enemy? Only one thing was sure: I wished all invaders gone from B. and everything as it used to be.

I want you to know that I was awake through all this; I wasn't dreaming. You're familiar, aren't you, with the old excuse that something went as fast as in a dream – bewilderingly fast, too fast to do the right thing. You would never let me get away with such an excuse. The more I equivocated, the more harshly you would judge me. Don't forget, though, that I am under no obligation to tell you anything. I could simply keep quiet and leave you in the dark. Apparently I feel moved to confess – for my sake, but I think also for yours.

Recently, when I was looking out the portrait of Vlad the Impaler for you, I found a little book that must have belonged to my great-grandfather, a leather-bound tome with gilt-tooled letters entitled *Dialogue between Socrates and Alcibiades: An Elementary Text on Self-Knowledge*. I skimmed it and then read it, and I felt it had been written just for me, especially the passage where Socrates says:

> *You have observed that the face of a person looking into the eye of another is reflected there as in a mirror, and this we call the pupil, for it is a kind of image of the person looking. The eye, then, need only look into another eye to see itself.*

I thought again of Traian, of how I'd squinted into his face from very close up, all because he'd said you were a liar if you kissed with your eyes shut.

But what image did he give off now, with flies buzzing out of his empty eye sockets?

I roamed through the nights, unable to get a clear picture of Traian's corpse; it fell apart whenever I tried to focus on it, like the thought that he was dead. Traian couldn't be dead. Mamargot was the one I'd always worried about. All my life I'd been afraid she would die. Her world, after all, was already gone; she alone remained, vulnerable and exposed, like in that poem, 'jutting solitary out of time, a loose rock in barren heights'.

But Traian?

Hi-da-day!

He had to be there, waiting for me somewhere.

And so one night I went to the cemetery with a bunch of flowers to look for his supposed grave. I had picked the flowers myself – blue wild flowers with a pale peony from our garden in the middle. It was the exact same bunch that Traian had once picked for me. Watching from my bedroom window, I'd seen him come into the garden with a bunch of blue flowers – and he'd spotted a pale peony at the side of the pebble path and stopped in his tracks, his eyes flitting back and forth between his flowers and this peony. I waited tensely behind the curtain to see if he would dare pick it. He reached out a hand – I saw him hesitate – and at last, with a swift, deft movement, he plucked it. He was about to add the peony to his bunch when Miss Sanda appeared and swiped at him with a long-handled broom.

'You mangy cur! How dare you? Just you wait, you scoundrel.'

Traian was off in a flash and Miss Sanda after him up the hill, her broom beating the ground behind her, *tack-tack, tack-tack*.

They both ran faster than they could, bent and stumbling, the flowers flying every which way.

I stood at the window for a long time laughing to myself. Later I laughed about it again with my friend Arina, who called Traian an idiot. I made a few sketches of the scene, but none of them was a success.

And now here I was with the bunch of flowers again! It was a splendid big bunch that I had picked by moonlight, and I couldn't wait to see Traian's face – an unusual desire, you might say, given the place where I was visiting him. I kept a lookout for a newly dug grave.

As I stepped briskly between the tombstones, the darting bats lifted my spirits. Did I feel any foreboding? All I know is that I hummed to myself and walked in three-four time: long-short-short, right-left-right, left-right-left. The tune was a song from the *Fledermaus* – the 'Bat':

> *Very funny, ha ha ha,*
> *Is the matter, ha ha ha,*
> *So forgive me, ha ha ha,*
> *If I la-augh, ha ha ha!*

Humming this, I waltzed towards the grave.

I didn't have to search for long. The earthy mound was on the left, not far from the entrance; I smelt it immediately. The strong scent of newly dug earth tickled my nose like musk.

I am not sure what happened next. A force rose inside me, pulling me up; my vertebrae clicked, and I felt strangely light and at the same time agitated about getting my turn. But at what? I was breathing through my mouth, sighing so hoarsely that it sounded like the trickle of distant scree – and then I was falling with the stones and the clods of soil, down onto this warm, earthy darkness that yielded, tickling and scratching me; I rolled around in the rising vapours, grunting and weeping and lowing, pressing my forehead into the earth and licking the little stones, taking them in my mouth and gargling with them, sputtering them out again.

Then I noticed a sour smell, and there before me were two of our security guards, in white traditional dress. Why the traditional dress? They ran away before I could ask.

I got up from the grave, shook off the earth and headed home, leaving the flowers with Traian.

The sun came up. I had no trouble staying awake, but my mood darkened. I put on my new sunglasses.

The dark lenses allowed me to retreat from that dazzling world that was so intent on revealing itself. I was no longer interested in seeing things except dimly, with Mamargot's gently drifting gaze.

We had breakfast in the garden.

Mamargot passed me the bread basket and I took the crust as always.

'Bon appétit,' Mamargot said to us. 'Do try Miss Sanda's strawberry jam.'

I could feel the change inside me, but told myself that all was as it used to be.

But which *used to* did I mean?

My blood was boiling again.

Geo was chatty that morning. He applauded the various cranes in B. that had flags flying from them: the Romanian flag, the jubilee flag to mark the country's centenary (some with a red-yellow-and-blue hundred), the blue flag of the EU and – quite unnecessary, Geo protested – the red flag of the Three Rose Party, to which Sabin, and presumably also Ata, belonged.

More flags flew from the tallest building in B., an abandoned four-storey eyesore up on the edge of the forest, not far from the old weaving mill. Once the local Communist headquarters, this building had been repurposed as the town hall after the fall of Ceaușescu and had stood under wraps ever since, supposedly awaiting renovation. Now the voluminous grey tarpaulin was hung with a vast picture of Prince Vlad the Impaler, so brightly lit at night that the nearby portable toilets were illuminated too.

Later in the morning we all walked up that way and stopped to look at this portrait which, somewhat superfluously, was also floodlit by day. Further up the road, meanwhile, in the souvenir kiosk, the same song played over and over:

> *All that she wants is another baby,*
> *She's gone tomorrow, boy,*
> *All that she wants is another baby, eh eh eh.*

Prince Vlad the Impaler stirred imperceptibly in the wind and we stood there as if rooted to the spot. Above the portrait, dripping red letters said *Dracula Park*, and two logos were emblazoned in the bottom right-hand corner – that of the Romanian Ministry for Tourism and the bat of 'Transylvanian Vampire Inc.'

'Ridiculous,' Mamargot said. 'Ludicrous! This *basse classerie* – they're ignoramuses, the lot of them.'

Ninel and I tried to calm her down; it wasn't good for her, we said, to get so worked up. Then we went on our way, but Mamargot kept raising her hand to her sunglasses, and every time, I felt that my eyes, too, were burning.

Here I break off writing, in two minds about whether to report our conversation to you – whether it's really neces-sary to your understanding of the story.

The fact was that Mamargot, as you know, was very much attached to this place, so that it was tactless of me, to say the least, to remind her that everything had an end, even our time in B. – that there was nothing to keep us here, nothing, indeed, to keep us in Romania.

Geo, unnecessarily, also stuck his oar in. He said it was a real tragedy that the young were going away. Mamargot reacted with unusual touchiness. Did B., she asked, mean nothing to me?

As we talked, the nasal voice of the Ace of Base singer continued to blare out non-stop from the souvenir kiosk:

All that she wants is another baby,
She's gone tomorrow, boy,
All that she wants is another baby, eh eh eh.

My only thought was how long ago it all was – the end of Communism, the nineties when this catchy song was a hit – and yet here in B. it was still playing on a loop at full blast, as if time had stood still.

But so what? What was the big deal? Why was I so on edge?

Up the hill in the cemetery, Ace of Base was still audible. Mamargot stopped to listen to a bird. What kind was it, she asked, had we heard it – but before I could reply, somewhat surprised, that it was only a blackbird, she was asking about Vlad the Impaler. Was there only one portrait of him? Why was it the same picture on all the posters?

She seemed to have put aside her annoyance, and glad of this, I told her what I'd learnt at school – that there were actually two pictures: a small fresco in a church, I'd forgotten where, and this famous portrait in the once fashionable three-quarter profile. Some claim to see in it the firm resolve of a just prince; others think they discern the cruelty of the Impaler.

Certainly, the portrait should never be considered out of context: the artist, a German at the court of Matthias Corvinus, has adhered strictly to Renaissance beauty standards, giving Prince Vlad a high forehead, a long, thin nose, big eyes with delicately arching brows, a pale complexion and a long, almost feminine neck. Hungarian and Turkish chronicles, however, describe him as short and stout with a furrowed, sunburnt face.

Here Mamargot laughed and, pleased to have amused her, I went on to explain that another important reference point for the German artist – presumably out of respect for our prince's Orthodox faith – was the art of the Byzantine church, with its elongated figures and staring faces, each with the fixed gaze of one who has the knowledge to do God's will. Again Mamargot was amused – but by now we had reached the newly dug, or perhaps redug, grave.

Stooping down, Mamargot glimpsed the corner of a wooden coffin.

'What kind of a farce is this?'

Ninel crossed herself with a giggle. 'It's the grave of that man,' she said. 'Traian Fifor.'

'My God,' said Mamargot, who was now peering at the concrete cross. 'Just look at this picture.'

Tacked to the cross was an oval-framed bust portrait of Traian in a brown suit and blue striped tie.

'The suit and tie are stuck on,' Mamargot said, laughing and crossing herself. 'And this blue sky round his head and the little clouds. It's all stuck on.'

'My God,' Ninel cried, 'that Sabin is a total failure.'

At the family vault we found two of the security guards, both in traditional Wallachian dress: white trousers, white shirts, hand-stitched shoes and broad leather belts with several rows of buckles.

I asked the reason for this festive attire and they confessed that they had received the clothes from the mayor's father. With the big influx of tourists, Mr Sabin had said, traditional dress would be an additional draw. It wasn't in breach of their contract, because we hadn't stipulated what they were to wear, or not to wear, on the job.

'But you won't let any tourists in,' Mamargot said.

They vowed to do no such thing.

'Be vigilant,' I said.

'Of course!' they said, 'That's what we're here for!'

I had a good look at them. They didn't seem to recognise me. But perhaps these were the other two.

I clapped one of them on the shoulder.

'Please be vigilant.'

In the courtyard of the grand ivy-covered house, tin tool sheds were being put up; beside them, a heap of sand bristled with shovels.

It was all go: builders effing and blasting, loud music, cheerful foremen, party cronies of Sabin, and thick smoke from an improvised barbecue. The Austrians were there too.

Now and then Mamargot peered across from the garden gate.

'We mustn't surrender this place, darlings,' she said. 'We mustn't let the *basse classerie* take over again.'

I promised I would always be there for her and she nodded – all this, she said, would one day be mine. She liked saying that, but it made me uneasy. Why couldn't she just come to Paris with me, when she was always banging on about how wonderful it was? Why did she never leave Bucharest except to go to B.?

I wanted to admire with all my heart whatever it was that Mamargot admired about this place, and so when the builders' racket had died down, I set up my deckchair under the lilacs.

It was already late afternoon.

I lay still for so long that all kinds of insects settled on me – even birds came and perched on my arms and on the arms of the deckchair. You would, I think, have been touched if you'd seen me; you would have thought I was lost in contemplation, at one with the place, the very picture of peace and serenity. In fact, my calm was a sign of the opposite; it was more like a numbness brought on by my violent dislike of B. and the world. My calm was a silently growing rage that I had yet to understand.

Behind my shades I pretended not to notice what was going on – pretended not to notice the noise re-emerging from the silence; the quivering hunger and greed that drove everything, even down at grass level; the crab spiders, yellow or white like the flowers where they lay in wait, invisible to their prey. In fact, despite the glasses, I saw more clearly than ever, and I heard – or so it seemed to me – the most infinitesimal of sounds, sometimes even before they were made. I found myself suddenly aware of the intentions of all living creatures – their sinister intentions, their avarice and malice, their relentless urge to pounce and kill. Was I still sane?

I saw a crab spider pull a big butterfly towards it with its ridiculously small pairs of legs and slowly inject its venom through its fangs.

I saw glow worms approach a snail and puncture its feeler eyes; I heard the froth bubble up and the snail writhe slowly in the grass and the sound of crushed sorrel stalks – and I pretended nothing was amiss. I pretended none of it was happening – or only in my imagination.

It was really very strange. I could see and hear more and more, but instead of delighting in these unhoped-for and supposedly artistic talents and putting them to use in my art, I cursed them and hoped they would go away if I ignored them.

I didn't even want to think about speeding up time by breathing more quickly or winking, because I was afraid of shortening Mamargot's life. I kept my eyes still behind the blue lenses and tried to think of Mamargot and her happy cries of 'Look how glorious!'

And yet I couldn't stop the changes in me, let alone reverse them. I saw and heard things I didn't want to see or hear, often without even trying. Lying quietly in the garden, I heard the ruthless march of ants and beetles and their fitful battle for whatever they saw as their inherent right.

It was the same in the air – and in the trees and on the white garden path. I knew, without having to look, that the mouse was stiff with shock beneath the blackbird's gaze. And in the bird's beady eyes I saw the stolid refusal of all beings to listen to the moans and whimpers and even the shrieks of the condemned.

Was all this necessary? Was it inevitable – a natural drive, a sign of vitality? And if so, didn't my inability to accept it show how out of touch I was with the world around me?

XII

We Be of On Blod

ABOUT THREE DAYS AFTER my senses had sharpened and I had become someone else, I saw Sabin's son, Ata, walk past the souvenir kiosk. I'd been lying in wait for him and pulled him towards me with my gaze. He came down the road to our gate and stopped, bewildered.

I was beginning to get used to my horrible new powers, but I was startled all the same.

'I suddenly felt I had to see you,' he said in the quiet, halting manner he always used with me.

'I know,' I said, deciding that I might as well be honest.

He stood there before me in a white shirt and black trousers – the shirt tapered, with the sleeves rolled up high.

'You haven't changed,' he said quietly.

He'd always talked to me like that – softly, to make me lean in to him. Now, though, I heard him loud and clear, and the leaning was only a sham.

'You haven't changed,' he said, raising his voice a little.

'That's nice of you,' I said. 'Thank you.'

I took a step back and contemplated him through my shades. The dark lenses made his skin look pale and his eyes and hair jet black. He might have been his own portrait – black chalk heightened with white on grey grounded paper.

Tina and Arina had both been in love with him as teenagers and suspected me of feeling the same – 'Just admit it!' Unlike the other men in B., they said, Ata had both feet on the ground; he would make something of himself. They had that from their mother, Auntie Ana. I for my part would roll my eyes and quote Mamargot, calling Ata a pale character, a man without passion – favourite epithets of hers to describe men she didn't think much of.

'Just admit it,' Tina and Arina would say, giggling. 'You like him too.'

Once they even said it in Ata's presence. We were walking past him and one of them pushed me towards him and called out in an unusually sharp voice, 'Admit it!'

I caught a hint of a smile on Ata's face.

Was it an indulgent smile? Or was there triumph in it?

He was a somebody, he had both feet on the ground. All the peasants in B. said so – maybe because, as the son of the most influential man in town (but unlike his busy dad), he wore his confidence with a certain lordliness. He held himself very straight and was never seen in company, resisted all friendship and had only occasional, very discreet liaisons with women – though they for their part were suspicious of his discretion and vied with each other in spreading shockingly intimate details of their affairs with him.

As a result, the legends surrounding Ata's phenomenal manly lust grew and grew, and disputes and sometimes even fights arose between the women, which only enhanced his reputation. I often wondered how a man without passion could evoke such passion in others.

Another thing about Ata: he had a striking interest in men's fashion. While all the locals were simply and shabbily dressed and went around barefoot or in plastic mules, Ata wore starched shirts and old-school waistcoats – for a time he even sported a panama hat. This concern for his appearance, combined with his solitary habits, touched the people of B. They liked Ata for being different from his father. He seemed to be informed about everything, and yet uninvolved, a profiteer who was above fighting for profit, a man who pretty much had it all – a chosen one, in his way.

Framed to his chest by our fence, he looked past me obliquely, presenting me with a three-quarter profile worthy of the glorious cinquecento and an impressive aquiline nose which, according to the humoral theory, is a sign of manliness, power and nobility. Behind his right shoulder, a long trail of ants, bathed in a mysterious glow, made its way up the rough bark of a fir tree, while behind his left shoulder, the road wriggled away into the distance, giving the picture depth and perspective, if nothing else.

Ata cleared his throat affectedly.

'Aren't you going to ask me in?'

'Sure, feel free.'

We sat down on one of the benches under the lilacs. He laughed his deep, throaty laugh and asked if I still played tennis.

'No,' I said. 'Not as much as I used to.'

'Why not?'

'I'm running out of partners.'

He laughed huskily again.

'I could play the odd match with you,' he said.

'I'm not in the mood,' I said. 'I'm not well.'

'Your aunt's death was a blow to you.'

'Not so much *her* death. It was Traian's that got to me.'

'Poor old Traian,' Ata said.

It wasn't that he made it sound as if he didn't care; it was the irony in his voice. Looking back, I'm sure it was that irony that made me so angry and that was, ultimately, Ata's undoing.

The wind soughed in the leaves. Somewhere nearby, a plank crashed onto cement, and further up the road at the souvenir kiosk a woman yelled, 'Awesome! Honey, this is so awesome!'

'You kind of liked Traian,' Ata said.

'Yes.'

'I'm sorry,' he said.

'That I liked him or that he died the way he did?'

We looked at each other, and when I smiled, Ata snorted with laughter.

'I've missed you,' he said, taking my hand.

At this point, Miss Sanda interrupted us with a plate of her homemade pies – spinach pies and nettle pies with lots of garlic. She put the plate on the garden table, together with a crystal carafe of water and blue glasses.

I see that carafe now as I write, sharp and clear against the pallid light, the glass misted with cold. It's as if it were here beside me – if I stop for a moment, I can almost feel the chill on the backs of my hands. It was water from the garden well.

Miss Sanda asked if she could bring us some coffee. Or some strawberry jam? Or a little of the rose-petal jam?

'No, thank you,' said Ata. 'We have all we need.'

She smiled contentedly and scuttled off again, turning at the door to tell us she was there if we wanted anything.

Then Geo came over to us. He was unusually warm towards Ata.

'Bye now, young man,' he said, clapping him on the shoulder. 'Take good care of the young lady.'

Ata rose to bid farewell to Mamargot and Ninel, and kiss their hands.

'Bon voyage!' he said. 'Go carefully on the road. It's full of potholes, I'm afraid.'

Mamargot and I exchanged amused looks. She was going to Bucharest to speak to a dependable lawyer and pay a brief visit to a doctor. Yunus would bring her back in a few days.

Ata and I waved to the receding car.

'Do you think Traian suffered awfully?' I asked.

'Stop thinking about it. There's no point.'

'What do you know about Traian's death?'

'Are you from the militia?' Ata asked, amused. 'Come on, eat with me.'

Was it lack of feeling or had he simply become more phlegmatic? If I'd painted him in that moment, I would have tried to capture the ambiguity in his averted gaze.

I poured him a glass of water and asked straight out whether he was as interested in our family vault as his father was.

'I'd rather hear about your blood ties with Dracula,' he said. 'You'd kept them pretty quiet.'

He leaned forward between the full glasses to kiss me.

'Just admit it,' I said. 'You're only doing this because you want access to the vault.'

'Oh God,' he sighed.

'Admit it!'

'All right, if you insist, I admit it all.'

We kissed; he tasted of garlic.

'This doesn't mean I'll grant you access,' I said.

He laughed. 'Why not?'

'Because it would be dangerous for everyone.'

'Dangerous? We could expropriate the vault. Ever thought of that?'

'That's not as easy as it used to be, believe me. That's not the danger.'

'So what is?' Ata sipped his water.

'Something quite different,' I said, meaningfully.

'But I love danger,' he whispered with an affected huskiness that oozed confidence. 'Don't you?'

'Oh yes,' I said. 'You bet.'

*

I have to confess that once Ata had left, I began to long for the night and for another of those dreadful encounters I was now familiar with. At the time, though, I couldn't have said *why* I felt such a longing – even trying to explain it now makes me so nervous that I lose the flow and forget what I'm trying to say. Maybe it's best if I stick to telling you what actually happened and let you make up your own minds – preferably each for him or herself, because we all know how self-righteous public judgments can be.

There I was, then, yearning for the night, looking almost lustfully at the fading light, the flashes of purple in the windows of the empty houses, the red glow on the cranes. The mountains were growing blacker and blacker and the forest was getting dark.

As night fell, the bats flew out with long sharp cries, while the heat rose from the dark gardens, heavy with the sweet breath of dying flowers. The moon shone over B., pale as an LED light on the roof of a grotto.

It was deathly still in the house when I went to bed, but every corner echoed with my scheme. It must have been past midnight. The damp, crumpled sheets chafed my skin. I was still awake, breathing fast.

More than once I thought it was about to happen, and I began to tremble, soothing myself with that childhood song, 'Johnny, tu n'es pas un ange'. I wondered why the woman didn't care whether or not Johnny was good – in fact, I almost fell asleep pondering the question.

The parallelogram of moonlight had shifted onto my covers, knocking the furniture awry. Its pale shaft stretched from the window to the bed.

I pretended I was fast asleep and seeing all this in a dream – even the one who came to me as shimmering green smoke, as thick clouds of pungent incense. It *was* incense, I would have recognised it anywhere. But the smell was so concentrated it was sweet – as if it were a cover for something else.

Then I became aware of a creeping sound on the walls and a sudden damp chill; in the heat of the summer's night I went cold and then hot, and I felt a tingling under my arms and between my legs, between my lips and in my mouth – wherever skin came into contact with skin, wherever the body was made to open.

I had heard him slip over the windowsill and slide slowly between the sheets, a long-drawn-out breathy sound that drowned my sighs.

'Come,' I said recklessly, though I spoke like one asleep. 'Come.'

And no sooner had I spoken than he threw himself upon me in the shape of a man – a weighty mass that I immediately embraced.

At the first touch I froze with horror. He was as smooth as a waxed marble statue, and as tepid too. I kept my eyes tightly closed and pulled my hands away. He smelt of incense and stale air, like that stuffed squirrel in the cellar – and also of copper, like some of Mamargot's necklaces. But his smell excited me all the same. I pressed my back into the mattress and arched my pelvis.

'Come,' I said, and soft, breathy sounds tickled my ear in reply, as dim as something from the bottom of a chasm.

I wanted to say something else, but a cold shudder ran through me, and when it reached my throat, I started up with a scream and threw back my arms.

I clung to his tepid body, pressing myself against it. Then I pushed him away and rolled over beneath him. He kept up the rhythm, as if his strength were a mere figment of my imagination.

I was exhilarated, hungry for rapture. Exhaustion, when it came, brought with it an unsated longing.

His body remained tepid, and so smooth that even my sweaty skin didn't stick to it.

We didn't kiss on the mouth – our faces slid off each other – but when I glimpsed his nipple through half-closed eyes, I latched onto it and sank my teeth in, and his blood spurted into my mouth, tepid and sticky on my tongue.

'We be of on blod,' he whispered.

I sucked at his nipple until he pushed me away and rose purposefully to his feet – a black shrouded spectre, grey in the moonlight.

'Don't go, please don't go!' I was trembling all over and wanted to say something else – but what? I didn't know. I wanted to quote from books, to speak of the woman who traced her lover's shadow on the wall – the origin of all painting.

I wanted to say something, but already he was silhouetted in the window frame, standing there alone, casting no shadow.

I grabbed him by his black cloak, but he was gone. Now I was the one standing alone at the window, a fistful of black smoke rapidly dispersing in my hand.

When I opened my eyes I was lying in bed in a
strangely twisted position so that I recognised neither the
room nor the layout of the furniture. My tongue tickled
in my dry mouth, as if I'd eaten too much garlic.

XIII

―――

From on High

W HEN HE'D GONE I WAS LEFT doubting whether he had ever been there, a numb sensation in all my limbs.

I ran to the window and jumped down.

It was like a dream and yet at the same time it wasn't; there was no ill-intentioned person who might have pushed me – and besides, I felt no fear. Down I went, headfirst, the wall of the house a choppy white sea beneath me, a loud rushing in my ears.

I clicked my tongue as I fell. Yes, I made that 'Ts' of displeasure, tossing back my head the way everyone does here – offhand, not even aware of what they're doing. *Ts*.

And as I tossed my head, I spun back up again; my belly skimmed the wet grass and I flew the other way. Twisting and turning, I slipped through the branches of the damp lilacs, then glided noiselessly over pump and fence and narrow path, and up the side of the first fir tree. A pair of collared doves fluttered out of the tree and flew off, flapping ponderously, but I felt as light and nimble as a stray thought. I no longer knew up from down.

As I travelled up the side of the fir, I moved my arms and legs as if I were climbing – although, of course, I was in the air and had nothing to push off from except my desire to make the best of my new powers. I felt no surprise and no enthusiasm either – only the urge to use this new energy to whatever purpose, preferably to the limits.

Once over the forest, I clicked my tongue again, rolled over onto my belly and began to make swimming movements, the pale moonlight on my back.

I headed away from town, not wanting to look down at B. – at the cranes and half-finished buildings, the TV crews' marquees and broadcast vans, the new lights everywhere which, seen from above, looked like a gleaming cobweb.

In a forest clearing I saw Ata's house, a misshapen villa very like ours, with a flower garden and two tennis courts. His dogs howled as I glided over it, and some of them jumped pointlessly over the fence.

I went on my way, still swimming naked through the air, my hair streaming out behind me. I should have felt cold, but I didn't. Nor were my eyes watering; nor was the wind roaring in my ears.

It looked rather as if the laws of nature no longer applied to me, and I accepted this with the same fearlessness with which, long ago, the Medieval Romanian heroes had accepted their fate. The treetops swayed in the breeze beneath me, and little brooks and rivulets reflected the moon a thousand times over in their rushing waters.

In the clearings, deer began to bay.

One roebuck belled so loudly and throatily that it seemed to be laughing at its own fear. Spittle sprayed as it belled louder and louder, its tongue protruding from its mouth.

I pounced down and sucked that laugh right out of it.

Between big sucking gulps, I hummed softly, and the creature's throaty whisper gave way to a long, peaceful moan. With one arm tightly round its throat, I heard it gurgle softly and then softer still until it collapsed on tangled legs.

Wiping the blood from my mouth and arms on its fur, I got up and clicked my tongue. And before I knew it, I was floating over the forest again. I kept a lookout for the river.

There it was, as bright as if it knew no night. Did it have a name? I'd never thought to ask. Grey boulders, veined with white, stood out with pin-sharp clarity in the water. The smell of fresh mint and dock filled the air, and bitter cress and purple loosestrife flowered on the banks, dwarfed by giant hogweed.

Patches of mist wetted my face as I flew through them.

When I moved on and the dew dripped off me, I felt as if I were crying.

Through the sickly-sweet smoke from the dump I saw bears, wolves and foxes, and – silhouetted against the moonlight on a branch – a squirrel that looked familiar to me.

I clicked my tongue again and sailed up the rockface, past slopes where firs clung on for dear life, over cascades of water, inlets and moorland, shelving rocks and ridges like bared teeth, black gaping passages into which no light penetrated. I soared through darkness and dim light, over the funicular cable that leads to the famous Romanian Sphinx and on to the Caraiman Cross that was built to commemorate our heroic ancestors. The strays on the fenced-in plinth sensed my presence; they sloped off, howling, knocking over aluminium cans that glinted in the night.

I glided down in the shadow of the cross with a sense of ceremony.

In spite of myself, I began to read the nickel plaques that had been put up by the Heroes Cult Association.

Queen Maria, I was informed, had had the cross erected after seeing the Carpathians in a dream, 'spattered with the blood of the heroes of the fatherland'. The cross was apparently at a higher altitude than any other of its size in the world.

I looked down at the open hilly countryside, the scattered villages and towns, the forest. Even B. was visible. I saw our villa, the dirt track, the other, more dilapidated houses that would soon be mutilated beyond recognition. I saw the gleaming cranes lit up in the dark and, further up the hill, the cemetery with its vaults and even – yes, there it was – our very own vault, burial place of the mighty prince and voivode, Vlad the Impaler.

I listened. It was quiet up here, night, awe-inspiring. From here the Wallachian warriors had launched attacks on their enemies. A breeze swept across the platform and blew through my hair. It must have been chilly, but although I was naked, I didn't feel the cold at all.

Slowly I raised my arms into the air, then called out over the Carpathians: 'Here I am, my prince!'

But it came out as a howl, like that of a wolf.

'Here! I!'

No, not the howl of a wolf – more like a hoarse bellow that broke into a wail. I heard it echo – but there was no reply.

I stood there for a long time, listening into the night.

Then I called again. Perhaps I was impatient. Everything inside me was squeezed out in another roaring howl that sent all living things fleeing for cover, and I lurched forward and threw myself after it – over mountain pines and rutted ridges, along the river, over firs and beeches and spruces and fleeing deer, over roads, cleared forest slopes and churned-up land, industrial estates, the glaring lights of the Schweighofer depot, tall stacks of timber, and then more fields, dark and crosshatched, more depots and wasteland.

Did I love this country as our forebears are said to have loved it? I glided past petrol stations, villages and factory ruins, past plastic tarps fluttering on the stalls of the vegetable markets – and I tried to match up what I saw with what I'd known in my youth.

I glided slowly past tower blocks with blue-lit windows, past flashing neon signs and over vast adverts for *MoneyTransfer* that loomed in the gardens of small loam houses. I sailed over beds of roses and the sweet tobacco

I used to call 'Queen of the Night', over asphalt ridged with tree roots, along poplar avenues – then over scattered houses again, the round roof of a well, benches, darkly gleaming chestnut trees. Above one loam house I even detected the pungent smell of burnt aubergine skins. My country!

Beneath me, a horse-drawn cart turned off the road, and the horses sensed my presence and shied. I soared over pylons whose tangles of black cables hung to the ground. I flew over the countryside with the diligence of a court messenger reconnoitring a land and its people, taking note of the mismanagement, the abandoned building sites, the cars parked haphazardly on the pavements, the absurd number of benches in the park, the rash of exchange bureaus and lottery kiosks.

As I chased a moth around the illuminated statue of a one-armed grenade launcher, mouth agape, an SUV rounded a bend below me with screeching tyres. I saw its anthracite-coloured roof and couldn't help myself – I had to jump.

I bounced a few times, like on a trampoline, and the roof buckled slightly.

The SUV stopped, but the engine kept running. I hovered two metres above the dented roof and heard the thudding beats inside being turned off. Then the door opened and a shorn-headed man with shades on his forehead got out unsteadily.

He walked around the car and examined the road.

'A dog?' a blond head called through the passenger door.

'You're a dog yourself and so is your whore of a mother!' the man called back.

He lay on his belly and looked under the car.

'But it was on the roof,' the blond head called out.

The man stood up, cursing, and peered over the roof.

'What the fuck!' He looked up in disbelief.

I entered his field of vision, a pale cocoon with splayed arms and legs. My black hair hung down over my face, my naked breasts swung, my fingers clawed at the air beneath me and turned to talons.

'Jesus Christ,' the man shouted. He shook his head and began to laugh.

'What's going on? Why are you laughing? You're always laughing,' the blonde woman said, and now she too got out of the SUV. The man jerked his chin at me and the woman looked up.

She looked at my naked body, then at the man, then back at me.

'Oh my God, you really are a dirty bastard,' she shouted after a while. 'I'm walking.'

She slammed the car door.

'Hey,' the man yelled, 'go easy on my car.'

I clicked my tongue at such *basse-classerie* and turned away.

But where next?

I drifted over roofs covered in fishbone antennae and satellite dishes, over the receding shapes of courtyards and allotments, maize fields and wheat fields, car parks, brightly illuminated malls and mechanics' workshops, over rolling hills and precipitously edged roads. I tried to read the lines beneath me.

Far below, in the water of a lake, I saw a rotting bridge. Then came more villages and I felt warmth on my belly as I flew over them, either from the life down there or from its putrefaction. Sickly-sweet smoke, rubbish everywhere, scattered or heaped or stacked, piles of rubble, low-slung shacks built every which way, cement yards, howling dogs and, on the other side of the hill, the wail of passing lorries, yellow and red lights, then silence again – a deserted, godforsaken place.

The sweet warmth rising up to me, the ubiquitous rot . . .

I clicked my tongue and immediately felt a pressure on my right shoulder and knew he was above me – or perhaps beside me, for there was no up or down, only a forward surge through the night; we were both heading the same way now, leaving burning fields and poisoned wells in our wake.

In vain was Mehmed II styled 'Abu al-Fatih', Father of the Conquest. To be sure, he led a mighty army, as big as that which took Constantinople. Armies of horsemen covered the field, Janissaries with lances, flags, arrows, sabres and yataghans, camels and artillery. But they advanced through empty, burnt-out country – everywhere the acrid smell of burning and no water. The wells had been filled with earth; there was no living creature far and wide.

The savages had laid waste to their own country and retreated, presumably into the mountains.

Then Mehmed's men came across a veiled woman in dirty white, sitting outside a ruined house and sucking a leather whip.

A good thing they'd come, she said. She could tell them all about the Wallachians – but first she needed to eat and drink.

A Janissary Aga took her on his horse and rode with her to the camp. He started to fondle her even before they arrived and was astonished to find her willing. He arranged for her to bath in his tent and change into clean clothes before he presented her to the sultan.

Such a beautiful woman, so disfigured, the sultan thought.

Then the plague broke out in the camp.

Many died, for the sick and feverish were immediately killed by their comrades, and their corpses burnt. People began to wash and drink more and more, lest they should appear heated and be thought infected. Water grew scarce.

Another cause for fear were the fleas that jumped off the corpses. Clothes and tents were burnt.

Everywhere the acrid smell of smoke and almost no water left.

Camels were culled and the famous cannon from the siege of Constantinople had to be left behind – buried so the Wallachians wouldn't find it.

Allah, succour us!

Troops of horsemen were regularly sent out to forage for victuals, but few returned.

Stay on the open field, avoid the tall grasses, avoid the moor, keep out of the forest. Don't go over the narrow mountain passes, for that's where Prince Vlad's formidable soldiers are lying in wait. Be on your guard and stick together; don't go out alone, not even to chase a deer or a hare. Don't go hunting. For you are the hunted.

And whatever they did, the sultan warned them, they mustn't slow down. Very soon, he said, the army would reach the Carpathians where there would at last be grass for the animals, little rivers, cooler temperatures.

It was searingly hot in the valley, even at night.

But on that godless night it was hotter than ever.

Not a breath of wind in the camp, the tents unstirring in the still air.

Then a chilling scream cut through the night – the scream of a victim or his executioner.

The sultan was already on his feet, curved blade in hand, when the barbarous hordes shot past his tent like a fireball. Battle cries and piercing shrieks rang out on all sides, and soon trumpet blasts, too, rent the air. Outside, the sultan saw Ottomans fighting Ottomans, Janissaries battling among each other, one Mohammedan striking another. And he cried, 'Shaitan! It's the devil!'

With bloody yataghans they mowed each other down, slicing off heads and arms and even animals' legs, while the drummers steadily beat the alarm.

Twisted, gaping faces, gory bludgeonings, flowing entrails, torches wielded like sabres, staring horses' eyes, men falling to their knees, corpses trampled underfoot, the battle scene a dark blur.

The sultan survived under a corpse – whether that of an Ottoman or a disguised Wallachian was never known. Too many had fallen – most of them, it is said, killed by the enemy's hand. When they lined up to continue their march, there were only half as many as before.

But the sultan refused to give up. With Allah's help he would prevail over this shaitan. It was only trying to frighten them, using its cunning to make them forget how slight its power.

His men dug trenches around the camp and drove stakes into the ground, and the Janissaries held meetings in their tents. They wore the white headgear known as Haji Bektash's sleeve and chanted their master's motto: 'Happy is he who sheds light on the darkness of thoughts.'

After days of strenuous marching, they came to the princely seat of Târgoviște. The cavalry, which had been sent on ahead, found the city deserted, but the sultan feared a trap and ordered his army to give the supposed ghost town a wide berth.

Meanwhile, however, a storm was brewing ahead, and the sky was darkening, though the air was no cooler – quite the contrary – and the stench of rotten food was growing stronger by the minute.

Some cool air at the foot of the Carpathians would be just the thing. Not long now and they'd be setting up camp there.

A drum roll set the pace for a quicker march. But at the sound of the drums the black clouds flew into the air – thousands of crows calling, 'Cra, cra, cra,' in their rasping voices and fanning a breeze so unbearably sweet and musky that even the most seasoned soldiers were shaken to the marrow.

'The forest!' one of them cried.

'The forest! The forest!' More and more of them took up the cry. And the drummers lost the beat, clattered and fell silent.

The sultan rode on ahead, so that he would be the first to see the mighty forest.

But there were no firs or beeches – only a forest of stakes hung with dead bodies.

The sultan trod so softly as he entered this ghastly forest with his grand vizier, the sultan's guard, the sultan's troops, and all the rest of his army – so softly that the crows flew back down and settled on the corpses. They perched on the hanging heads and skewered shoulders and flew into the dead men's chests which were alive with a great fluttering and cheeping.

Skeletons stared down at the sultan through empty eyes, and bared their teeth, while everything else drooped off them: shreds of putrid flesh, tattered clothes, cracked bones. Sounds of buzzing filled the air. Fat flies cut through the tableau and settled on polished armour.

Around the edge, the stakes were smaller – so small that some of the skeletons touched the ground. But the deeper you penetrated into this infernal forest, the taller the stakes, and on the very tallest of these, the sultan – pressing the end of his turban to his nose to keep off the smell – was astonished to discover himself, Sultan Mehmed II, Abu al-Fatih, wearing the very turban that was on his head!

Did his grand vizier also see this monstrous thing? Did the warriors see it?

The sultan began to laugh.

The others joined in; the laughter became uproarious.

'Shaitan!' the sultan cried. 'The man is a devil!'

And still laughing, they turned and fled.

XIV

Ordo Draconis

A T THAT TIME, DRAWING WAS the only thing I did as a matter of routine. I took my sketchpad and pencils with me wherever I went – usually to the cemetery, where I'd been going every day since Mamargot's departure.

Imagine this landscape: a hill with tall, windswept grasses, yellowing here and there and russet – the colours alone enough to evoke the scent of hay and the sound of crickets; the vaults on the hillside reminiscent of shepherd's huts. But what is this? Outstretched arms, indecently sunburnt, jut into the air all over the place, and hands curl around phones, poised for selfies: one with the grave, one with the epitaph – hundreds of selfies with the crooked crosses.

Selfies outside our vault, selfies with the funny men in traditional dress – these people were cynical self-promoters, frantically chasing the ultimate weird photo. But they laughed all the time, as if they didn't take their photography seriously.

'This is so awesome.'

'Yeah!'

'But guys, guys, wait a moment – where's Vlad?'

'Would you like a picture of yourself as Vlad the Impaler?' I asked, sketchpad under my arm, like in Montmartre in my Paris days.

My first sitter was a Dutch tourist in his mid-twenties. I caricatured him in the style of Jan van Eyck, capturing his likeness by violently distorting his features: a broad peasant's face, a low, bulging forehead, rather small eyes and a turned-up nose with very visible nostrils. He had shaven temples and a Samurai braid. I asked him to untie his hair; it hung to his shoulders.

'That's better,' I said.

He looked at me expectantly.

I added Vlad the Impaler's features to his picture, taking the famous portrait as my model. I lengthened his forehead by pushing back the hairline, arranged his hair more closely about his face, made his nose more aquiline and enlarged his eyes.

'You have a lovely mouth,' I said, 'just like Prince Vlad's.'

It was the truth. There was no denying the similarity.

The man was delighted.

I passed the money he paid me straight to our security guards.

In fact, I gave them all the money I made from the portraits. That way, I thought, they wouldn't forget who they were working for.

And so the vault remained closed to tourists, while the demand for 'Dracula-style' portraits soared. I don't think it would be wrong to claim that those portraits I drew in the cemetery were the sole Dracula attraction in B.

Everyone got to discover their hidden resemblance to Dracula. And as I drew, sitting on a grave or bench, or even on the ground, I began to talk about the Impaler. People were grateful. At last, they thought, a local who would give them the true story of the legendary Prince Vlad without resorting to the tricks of a tourist scammer like Sabin.

Dracula – they called him that even back in the days when he ruled over Wallachia. His father was a Dracula. The name was a byword for loyalty and integrity.

The story goes like this: when Prince Mircea the Elder died after many years on the throne, there came a time of disruption and disorder. For thirty-two years he had steered the fate of Wallachia with a steady hand; the Burgundian Chronicles called him 'the most courageous and capable of all the princes of Christendom'. A number of wise alliances had enabled him to bring peace to the region – he was the most trusted partner of Sigismund of Luxembourg, King of Hungary, and paid symbolic tribute to the Ottoman Empire for his country's independence. He encouraged trade, minted coinage that was used well beyond the frontiers of Wallachia and was a friend of liturgical music and ecclesiastical painting. His many children were raised on the same peaceable principles by which he governed: a ruler should provide for good neighbourly relations and general prosperity, and must spread the Christian doctrine.

You will wonder how it could happen that after such a long period of harmony, war should break out again so suddenly – petty feuds and sordid disputes over the throne. The powerful landowners or boyars all sided with different sons and nephews of the late prince, depending on where their interests lay. They travelled to neighbouring countries, broke alliances, forged others – and before long the fighting had spilt over into the rest of the region. For sixteen years, various men of straw took their turns on the Wallachian throne. The people suffered, the boyars sank into poverty – at one point the region was even governed by a ruler known as 'Praznaglava', the Empty-Headed.

Meanwhile, at the court of Sigismund of Luxembourg, now King of Germany and Holy Roman Emperor, there lived a wise and good-natured young man by the name of Vlad, a son of the late Prince Mircea. This Vlad reminded Sigismund of his old ally; he took a liking to the young man and made him a member of the Ordo Draconis.

Only a few select monarchs and noblemen belonged to the Order of Dragons: the kings of Poland, Serbia, Lithuania and Aragon and a handful of Polish and Hungarian magnates. These men swore eternal friendship to each other and vowed to stand by one another everywhere in the cause of good.

For young Vlad, this was a dream come true. He took his oath in Nuremberg and received a gold medallion embossed with the order's emblem: a coiled-up dragon symbolising the triumph of humility over chaos, and above the dragon, a cross that bore the words *O, quam misericors est Deus* on its horizontal beam – 'O, how merciful is God' – and on its vertical beam, *Justus et pius* – 'Just and pious'.

When, thanks to the diplomacy of his fellow order members, Vlad became prince of Wallachia, he had the dragon and cross stamped on the coins, so that everyone in and beyond the borders of the land would know of the change. All the churches he founded were likewise decorated with the cross and the coiled-up dragon – and because the Latin for dragon is *draco*, the Wallachians called their prince Dracula.

Vlad Dracula père, who bequeathed both Christian and surname to his more famous son, has gone down in the history books as a wise and mild ruler. To his three sons, Mircea, Vlad and little Radu, he was a living example of the principles of the Ordo Draconis – pious, just and above all merciful to his people.

It was his aim to maintain peace by means of peace, and for a time he was successful.

But Wallachia was caught between Hungary and the Ottoman Empire, and before long those two great powers were locked in a bitter war.

When the sultan's powerful army crossed Wallachia, Prince Vlad made speed to meet it and begged clemency for his people. He asked that peasants, shepherds and boyars be protected from pillaging and their lives spared. In exchange he offered food, and promised to remain well-disposed to the sultan.

Then, not wanting to take sides, he pledged loyalty and friendship to the new Hungarian prince.

But this indiscriminate friendship pleased neither of the warring parties.

Vlad and his sons were taken prisoner and brought to the sultan's court. Here an admonitory execution was to be held and the prince's fickleness cruelly punished.

The only way, Vlad was told, was through Allah, who revealed himself to his people through their ruler. The ruler was the first to follow that way and must follow it without fear. The sultan had many sons, all loved and cherished, but the law provided for only one ruler with undivided power. And so the Sultan must choose the most capable of his sons to succeed him, and when that son ascended to the throne, he must have all his brothers killed.

But that could never be God's will, Vlad Dracula protested.

The sultan was astonished by this bold utterance from one who would soon be dying in agony, and he invited the prince to join him and the grand vizier on the divan. They talked and talked, drinking coffee and speaking Greek like the educated elite and – like Sigismund of Luxembourg before him – the sultan took a liking to this steadfast Wallachian who seemed to trust in some special grace of God. But the grand vizier declaimed: 'O the depths of the riches both of the wisdom and knowledge of God! How unsearchable are his judgments, and his ways past finding out! For who hath known the mind of the Lord? or who hath been his counsellor? Or who hath first given to him, and it shall be recompensed unto him again? For of him, and through him, and to him, are all things to whom be glory forever. Amen.'

Would the prince like to see the sultan's palace?

Gladly, said the prince.

And so the sultan took him all round the gardens, pavilions and stables, showed him his collection of arms, including those of Mohammad and the first caliphs, and ended his tour at the palace school where the young men were trained in the clerical professions – all boys from the subjected territories. For the sultan's loyal Janissaries had been born the children of Christians and were the fruits of the annual 'boy harvest' in the Balkans.

Then the sultan called for his sons and introduced them to the Wallachian prince one by one, finishing with Mehmet, his chosen boy, the future sultan. The boy, who was smaller than many of his brothers, smiled at the prince. He was twelve and, like all beloved progeny, he was a trusting child.

Had the prince decided which of his sons would succeed him on the throne, the sultan asked. Assuming, of course, that he was pardoned.

The eldest, said the prince.

The sultan nodded thoughtfully and immediately decided that the prince should be pardoned and his eldest son with him. He would let them return to Wallachia as soon as they had sworn eternal loyalty to him. The two younger children, however, must stay behind in one of his palaces as tokens of their father's loyalty. Vlad was eleven at that time and his brother Radu was five. They would benefit from the excellent education of the Ottoman elite.

And so young Vlad and Radu said goodbye to their father and remained at the sultan's court. That afternoon,

Mehmet took them under his wing and introduced them to the other children.

I had quite an audience. I remember one woman opening a bottle of Nivea Sun as she listened and jumping at the snap of the lid as if she were at the theatre.

Where did I get all these stories, she asked. Was it part of my study course?

I told her I'd picked them up here and there. It was always a good idea to explore your own heritage.

And what happened next to Vlad Senior?

He continued to reign for a few years, remaining loyal to the Hungarians and backing the crusaders in their battle against the infidels together with his son Mircea. When the crusaders fired at the Turkish strongholds on the Danube, however, Prince Vlad is said to have cried, because the strongholds had been built by his father and were surely the last of such beauty. When the Hungarians heard this, they suspected him of a secret alliance with the Ottomans and sent an army that killed him and his son Mircea.

Vlad Dracula Junior, his later-to-be-famous son, was seventeen at the time. He asked the sultan's permission to claim his father's inheritance and assume the throne of Wallachia.

The sultan let him go, but offered no help when Vlad was dethroned soon afterwards by an adversary who was favoured by the powerful boyars. This man had shown great humility towards the sultan and paid him high tribute. He kept the boyars sweet, too, by lavishing money and gifts on them. Having arrived at the source from which all money flowed, he could pay out all there was to pay.

Vlad was greatly grieved by the corruption of them all.

For eight years he travelled around. First he stayed with the prince of Moldavia; then, when the prince was murdered, he fled Moldavia with his cousin Ştefan, travelling through Wallachia to Transylvania, and on to the Hungarian court.

The Hungarian courtiers were all greatly struck by this outcast who behaved so nobly and held himself so stiffly, and yet jousted with such spirit. They were astonished, too, that a young man who had grown up in the sultan's palace should be so outraged at the fall of Constantinople. While the talk at court was all of the future – of the flow of trade and the toll to be levied at the border between Transylvania and Wallachia – young Vlad knew only one topic: Constantinople! Was it possible that he was a devout Christian? Had he remained true to Orthodoxy? His brother Radu, they knew, had converted to Islam; there were close ties of affection between him and the sultan, and he was known as Radu the Handsome.

Meanwhile the king of Hungary fell into a dispute with Vlad's adversary over the tolls at the passes into Wallachia. The king wanted the Transylvanian Saxons to rearm the old fortifications in exchange for toll rights, so that the Hungarian border would be protected from the Ottomans. But the incumbent prince of Wallachia was against tolls, and so the king of Hungary decided to replace him with a man he could trust – Vlad Dracula!

So it was that in 1456 Vlad Dracula was at last made prince of Wallachia.

By then he was twenty-five and impatient to rule. He spoke fluent Romanian, Turkish, the Ottoman Turkish of the elites, Greek, Hungarian and a smattering of German. He was also a skilled horseman and could fight with all the weapons of his time.

'Holy shit!' yelled the Nivea Sun woman, when I handed her the portrait I'd done of her. 'I'm badass Dracula!'

XV

Dracula the Impaler

'**H**E WAS AN HONEST RULER, a tough guy with a strong hand.'

That resonated with my audience.

A new era dawned with Vlad Dracula, a truly Draculan era. He did credit to the Ordo Draconis, harnessing the chaos of the world, starting in his own country.

For eight years he had travelled around, surveying the state of things. He was now acquainted with Wallachia and the bordering countries; he knew all about the boyars and their peasants and serfs; was familiar with the nomadic shepherds, the merchants and the carousing populace, the priests who preached one thing and practised another, the egoism of the powerful and the selfishness of the pesky beggars on the markets, the travelling puppet shows and the nation's love of crude jokes.

There he was, on the throne of a country that took neither itself nor the throne seriously. The first thing he had to do was establish order.

My listeners nodded – they knew what I was talking about. It was the same where they came from.

Apart from the venal boyars, who switched princes as the mood took them, the country was impoverished. There was no stability. With each new government, all the old was swept away: trade plans, alliances – it was a mess. The powers that be were interested only in plundering their subjects. 'This country is like nowhere else,' people said, and decided that stealing from thieves was not a vice but a virtue. Before long, thievery was rampant.

Pity the poor traveller! No sooner had he dismounted his horse than the horse thieves were upon him; no sooner had he sat down to eat than the artful whores and pickpockets began to circle – and what they didn't take would be nabbed by the wily landlord. You couldn't rely on officers of the law unless you were rich enough to pay for justice. The thieves knew that and were ruthless. And so the traveller would set off again, a horde of stinking, mewling beggars in his wake, baring their putrid wounds and self-inflicted mutilations.

A cursed place, this! The people spineless, without a crumb of honour. A sneering insult to the great princes of the past, an insult to this beautiful region with its mountains full of gold, its rich salt deposits, its fertile fields.

He, Vlad Dracula, would drive their sneers out of them!

There he stood with his still unrecognised power and his unshakable will to serve the dragon – young Vlad Dracula, great prince and voivode, sole ruler, chosen by God to rule over all Wallachia!

Be just and pious – such had been his father's instructions. But where should he put his faith? Not even the Christian allies could be relied upon. Hadn't Christendom looked the other way when Constantinople was besieged and destroyed? Bold-faced Mehmet had been able to ride his horse into the Hagia Sophia with no cause for fear. Where had the European rulers been then? People showed courage only towards the weak; they did nothing to oppose the powerful. Was that justice? He'd show them justice!

Justice was the upright stake of the cross, connecting heaven and earth. He, Vlad Dracula, would drive this stake through the heart of his country with such force that all the world would tremble, to the glory of God.

I scanned the reactions of my audience. Understanding nods all round. They were all with me.

As soon as Dracula took the throne, the powerful boyars came from far and wide to hail him. They all wanted to be first; they all wanted to be closest to the new prince. And although it was Lent and he wasn't eating meat, Prince Vlad held a banquet for them.

There was much eating and drinking and jubilant toasting of the new prince. Spirits were high.

'How many princes has Wallachia had before me?' Prince Vlad asked.

'Seventeen!' one of the boyars cried.

Laughter.

'Wrong!' cried the young prince.

'Twenty!' another called.

'Ts!'

'Thirty-two!' called yet another.

'You haven't a clue about our history,' Prince Vlad shouted, and he laughed. And the boyars laughed too.

But Prince Vlad rose and ordered them all to be impaled. Then he had the banquet carried out into the courtyard and dined among the impaled men.

His page, who was with him, held his nose to keep out the stench of the dying men. When the prince saw this, he gave orders that he, too, be impaled – on a tall stake, so that he wouldn't smell the stench.

How did this impalement business work, the tourists asked, and I made sketches to show them. The tip of the stake was greased to make it slippery, and the condemned person was pulled onto it in a lying position. Ideally, it was inserted into an existing hole, then carefully knocked in with a mallet, past the kidneys and heart, and out at the mouth – or through the throat, between the victim's head and shoulders. After that, the stake was lifted up and stood upright – like a tree with a weird fruit hanging from it.

My audience chuckled and took photos of my sketches. They liked anything freakish, anything that didn't bore them. The Impaler would have been face to face with his victims, I told them; the stakes weren't usually very tall. Sometimes the impaled would slide down a little on their blood, their mouths oozing vomit – or even faeces that had been driven up by the stake.

As the tourists listened, I saw them gripped by a kind of vicarious frenzy that eventually gave way to a state of blissful languor.

If Vlad Dracula seemed bloodthirsty, I told them, it was because we tended to rank life higher than our beliefs and morals. To my amusement, they agreed with me.

When the common people heard of the brutal death of the grasping boyars, they cheered and sang the praises of the new prince.

'Hosanna!' they cried as he rode through the gates of Târgovişte, and they spread cloaks and willow branches on the road in front of his horse.

Rather than dressing in a lavish boyar's coat, the prince preferred to wear a coat of mail, like the Saint George of the icon painters.

And hardly had Vlad been made prince than he was visited by a legation of the Sultan to remind him of his tribute. He received the men in his throne room in the presence of the entire court and asked them to bare their heads after the custom of the country.

Take off their turbans? Never! the emissaries said. Their faith forbade it, as Prince Vlad well knew.

'Your faith!' said the prince. 'Indeed!' And he laughed.

In that case, he said, he would make sure that their turbans were correctly positioned.

And he gave orders for the turbans of the Ottoman emissaries to be nailed to their heads with three large nails apiece.

This bold deed elicited more cheers from the populace.

My listeners were also impressed. 'Hurray!' one of them yelled.

Prince Vlad wasted no time in getting together a valiant army. He had no riches to give his soldiers, but great honour and glory. Only the bravest of the brave were encouraged to join; he made quite clear that there was no place for cowards under his command. And soldiers came from far and wide; some of the recruits who swore eternal loyalty to him were as young as fourteen.

They all wanted to see Vlad the Bold, and he was exactly as people said: modestly dressed, but as tall and straight as a saint on an icon; prudent-minded, but unbending in his judgment – the legendary dragon slayer, wild and just! His gaze was steady, his gestures confident; his cry came from deep in his chest and was said to drown even the clank of sabres.

He oversaw his men's training himself and spoke to everyone, regardless of rank. He was the best cavalier in the land and skilled with all weapons. He also proved a tireless teacher.

In battle he rode fearlessly at the head of his army, broke through the enemy line and made straight for the Ottoman commander, leaving a broad swathe of destruction in his wake.

The history books tell us that his small army triumphed on all fronts and drove back the aggressor.

And word spread through all the land that Prince Vlad examined his injured soldiers in person after every battle. If their injuries were on their backs because they were cowards who had turned and fled the enemy, he had them impaled; but if they had injuries on their chests or faces, he praised them for their courage and admitted them to his circle.

'Worthy is he, worthy is he,' the Orthodox priests chanted.

Then one day he appeared before the populace with his bride, and there was a great throng of people wanting to touch him just as they might touch a saint's relics in the hope of being blessed.

'Hosanna!' the people cried.

And the many beggars in the crowd hoped for a shower of gold coins.

But the prince's guard rebuked the throng.

When the prince heard this, he was indignant. 'Suffer the needy,' he said, 'and forbid them not, to come unto me.'

His guard dispersed the blockade. Then the scruffy beggarfolk threw themselves at his feet, and words of praise rose from toothless mouths.

And the prince gave orders that these people be admitted into the big festival tent to partake of the wedding banquet.

He and his bride took their seats at the end of the table and dined with them.

'These are my people,' Prince Vlad said to his bride, a Transylvanian noblewoman whom he had married on the recommendation of the King of Hungary.

And his bride bit back her tears and ate, averting her gaze from such ugliness.

Meanwhile the red wine flowed in abundance, and the beggars cheered and toasted the bride and groom. Might they have many children, all as brave as the prince.

Then Prince Vlad asked, 'Would you like me to rid you of your cares, that you may henceforth want for nothing?'

And the beggars cried with one voice, 'Yes!'

So Prince Vlad left the wedding tent with his wife and gave orders for it to be set on fire from all sides.

And when his wife and her court ladies saw this and heard the screams, he said, 'I did this that they might no longer suffer or be a burden unto others. May there be no more poverty in my land, but only plenty.'

This incident, too, got about among the populace. And although people were afraid, they were pleased to have so bold a ruler – and delighted that Wallachia was being cleaned up. The next generation, they told themselves, would have it better. Without Prince Vlad, the place would have continued in this pitiful state for another few centuries, populated by beggars and thieves and despicable leeches. But the prince tore out the bad, roots and all.

Lack of honour was so odious to him that he had any thief, fraud or other wrongdoer immediately executed, usually by impalement. None of the condemned could buy themselves free, however rich they might be. There was only one justice, for everyone.

Sometimes one of the tourists listening to me would shake their head, and I would say, 'You don't have to listen – no hard feelings if you get up and go.'

It was a brutal story, after all, and not an easy one to hear – the story of a man who had looked the monster in the eye and held its gaze. It is given to only a few to see the wickedness of the world and its unspeakable suffering without letting it distract them, but Prince Vlad had the great power to look the monster in the eye without blinking or lowering his gaze. Soon it was the monster who was looking Prince Vlad in the eye – and the monster was startled by what it saw.

'I, great voivode and prince, sole ruler, appointed by God to rule over all Wallachia!'

When previous princes had given orders, they had threatened the disobedient with dying out of favour with the Holy Virgin. When Prince Vlad gave orders, he simply said tersely, 'It shall not be otherwise,' and everyone hastened to obey.

I told of his daring battles and the great feats of his small army, and everyone listened spellbound.

Before long he had defeated the dragon abroad and at home. There wasn't a thief left in Wallachia. Merchants could travel untrammelled day and night, sleeping in forests and leaving their money bags unattended with no fear of being robbed. The prince had golden cups left by the wells for everyone to drink from, and no one stole them.

The day that one of those cups went missing, there was no doubt in anyone's mind: something had happened to the prince!

The weekend before Mamargot's return I was sitting in the cemetery telling people about the justice of Prince Vlad and the awe in which he was held, when Ata came by with party president Druga and a heavy escort of large men in suits.

It really was Druga. It was the first time I'd seen him close up. He was smaller than I'd expected, but I recognised his grey moustache and bad teeth and his habit of saying 'the whole shebang'. He greeted us as a group – he and Ata were the only ones to bother with greetings.

'Hello!' he said. 'We thought we'd come and take a look at the whole shebang.'

'Hey,' Ata called to the tourists. 'Do you know who you've been talking to? This lady here is a descendant of Count Dracula! Her family owns the vault with his grave. Maybe she'll let us in to see if he's there – or if the coffin's empty ...'

Now he had them eating out of his hand. Druga clapped him on the shoulder.

'Really?' the tourists asked.

They begged me to open the vault.

'All right,' I said. 'Come on then.'

I don't know why I agreed. Was it because I'd been put on the spot? Or was I angry? My stories clearly weren't enough for these people; they were thirsting for more. Well, go on down then, if that's what you want, happen what may ...

I asked the flummoxed guards to open the tomb.

They rolled up the sleeves of their traditional white shirts, lifted the heavy marble slab with a groan and pushed it aside.

Someone claimed to have seen green smoke.

There was laughter at the thought.

And again that blissful shudder.

'Down you go, ladies and gentlemen,' I said. 'Who's first?'

I looked at Ata.

'All right,' he said roguishly. 'Why not?'

Druga clapped him on the shoulder again.

I can see it all now – Ata climbing down into the vault, his handsome hands gripping the third rung from the top, his knuckles white. He can't have been far from the bottom. I hear a breeze shiver through the trees and a rustle of dry grass. Then that dull thud down below that the others don't seem to have heard – but by then he was out of sight, and all we could see was the hard-packed earth on the floor of the vault.

The tourists had formed a queue to go down behind him. They made a good backdrop for Druga and the men in suits who were taking photos of themselves with the security guards.

'Would the lady in shorts mind getting out of the picture, please? This is a cemetery, you know.'

Someone asked if I had candles in the vault.

One of the large men went off to pick wild flowers, but ended up, amid general hilarity, plundering the other graves instead.

Druga meanwhile was standing a little way off, having a smoke with another of the large men. The grave, he was saying, wasn't so important to the whole shebang – the theme park with the recreated village, the castle, the ghost train and all the rest of it. On the other hand, if you looked at the whole shebang, the grave might actually be important. It depended. Either way, they needed to be clearer about what they wanted. They needed to make some headway. The companies were up and running, the lobbyists had been taken care of – he wanted to see results. He wanted a bit of action at the country's centenary. Otherwise they could forget about the next elections and that would mean losing the judiciary again. None of the comrades wanted that! It would send the whole shebang back to square one, for Christ's sake.

He spoke through pinched lips, smoking in long drags with his eyes closed. Then he dropped his arm stiffly, his hand in a loose fist, as if he were trying to conceal the cigarette.

Finally he tossed the butt in the dirt and ground it out with his foot.

Time to get going, he said.

One of the guards asked me if he should check on Ata. 'Ts!'

'Time to go, Ata,' one of the besuited men yelled into the vault.

'Servus,' Druga said, maybe thinking he was in Transylvania, where that's what you say for goodbye. And he left with his escort.

Only the man who had shouted into the vault remained. He shouted again. 'Come on, Ata, the others have already gone.'

But there was no answer.

'Does it go far underground?'

'Ts! Not that far.'

We waited.

The people in the queue grew alternately nervous and amused at their own nervousness.

'You okay, mate?'

They listened.

No answer.

One of the guards said he'd better go and have a look – the poor guy might have fainted or something.

'Please don't go down there,' I said.

I see us all waiting, the guards standing to attention, arms folded across their chests.

Was Ata a prankster, they asked. Because it was their job to guard this property here, wasn't it?

'Come back up now, Ata,' I shouted. 'Or we'll lock the vault and leave you inside.'

I blinked the time away until I saw Ata's head reappear in the opening of the vault – his gelled hair. He pulled himself slowly up the ladder, swaying slightly.

When he reached the top, everyone peered into his face to see if he was pale.

He blinked in the light.

'Don't go down there,' he said dazedly. There was all this green gas, he said, and the stench – it couldn't be healthy.

Meanwhile the guards pushed the stone back into place. Was it unhealthy to guard the vault, they asked.

'No,' I said. 'No need to worry.' Ata, I explained, was just trying to make it more interesting to the tourists.

The guards nodded as Ata made a hasty exit. The tourists, too, hurried away. Only the guards remained, concerned about their health.

Perhaps it was the strong ancestral blood ties that allowed me to be privy to events I had never experienced. For I could, it seemed, make the past present again. Whether this process was akin to empathy or more like a sort of retrospective voyeurism was not something I stopped to ask myself.

I didn't mourn either, not even when I recalled my own transience, for I was on my way to acquiring the indifference of the brave. I saw that indifference in the balance of colours that I managed to recreate – even down in the cellar, under the low-hanging lightbulb. My arm knew the routine; it remembered the proportions – and I used colour to bring them out: the narrow face framed by dark hair, the pale complexion, the curved brows arching down to the nose, the throat exposed by the open collar. I even painted myself a red velvet coat with clunky gold buttons on the breast.

I stood to paint under the buzzing lightbulb that lit up the rising dust, surrounded by dusty things that I'd assumed had been thrown out long ago – all that unwieldy Communist-era furniture piled high and deep with stuffed animals, oil cloth, macramé, tapestries, curtains, long-fringed pennants, ashtrays in polychrome Plexiglass, wicker baskets filled with plastic oranges, mustard jars, fan heaters, artificial roses in lacquered vases, lamps with frosted-glass shades. In the absence of a dump in B., it was all still here – the rolled-up synthetic rugs, the glass-fronted ornament cabinet with sliding doors, a dusty grey Cinderella with only one shoe, a hoopoe, a pair of street urchins in a fight, a cock and hen, a petrol-blue horse and that fisherman with a glass perch at the end of his line. All these things, which I had only ever seen fleetingly as they were carried out, were now all around me as, purposefully and with a sure hand, I painted my self-portrait, without a mirror.

I painted with a confidence that was new to me, as if I were following predetermined lines. My white hand slid across the canvas like a stranger's, and yet it moved with my approval. Never before had I been so sure of my art, of its unequivocal message.

When I was finished, I went to the wardrobe, which had a key in the lock hung with a red, yellow and green pompom.

I opened the wardrobe and found, as I had hoped, a mirror on the inside of the door.

Its light, a quivering parallelogram, skimmed the junk and shone into my eyes. I looked at the easel and then back at the mirror to see if I resembled the painting.

I screamed at what I saw. The shock made me crumple to the ground.

The horror!

It was as if I were suddenly alone, far from all things.

And yet at the same time I was no longer there at all.

I had descended from quite substantial confidence to a complete lack of substance.

I pulled myself up to the mirror and peered into it once more. But I had seen right – there was nothing but a collection of bibelots: the hoopoe, a hare, a drunk with a raised bottle. It was the junk behind me, the dust still glittering in the light. There was no reflection of me! Not even when I went over and picked up the ornaments. They hovered in the air, apparently floating – the hare and the hoopoe and the drunk, swaying back and forth as if they could fly. I dashed them to the floor and returned to the mirror, this time approaching it from the right, with the lightbulb behind me.

I could see the bulb in the mirror, but although I was standing with the light behind me and the mirror in front of me, there wasn't so much as a shadow reflected in the glass.

The world I knew was retreating from me – and yet I was still in it.

But who was I? I returned to the self-portrait on the easel and studied it closely.

Yes! It was the portrait of Prince Vlad the Impaler. The picture I knew so well.

Only it was no longer turned away in three-quarter profile, but looking right at me, straight into my eyes.

XVI

The Night Attack

I COULD SMELL THEIR FEAR and apologised – I hadn't meant to frighten them.

'No, no,' they assured me. 'No problem.'

They rubbed their rough hands and rocked from one leg to the other to ease their scared stiffness.

I'd caught them changing shifts; they'd been talking to each other. But they hadn't been smoking and they hadn't been drinking either. All four were of good Transylvanian morals – positively German.

'This is the grave of Prince Vlad Dracula,' I said. 'And God has chosen you to serve him.'

They were standing to attention again, their thick necks and burly arms silhouetted against the moonlight.

'Wait here,' I commanded.

I flung the marble slab effortlessly aside as if it were a light duvet, and lowered myself down the ladder.

Once at the bottom, I began to walk, though without seeing where I was going. Was I moving forwards or downwards, into a chasm or even on the roof of another tomb?

My long black hair hung down, the only pull on my weightless body. Then I felt something solid under my palms – clods and stones, twisting roots as thick as arms, and finer ones like hairs.

Something shimmered in the distance and I made my way towards it, keen and bold as a young soldier. It seemed so close and was yet so far. A cloud of sickly-sweet incense went up amid murmurs and sighs, but I still had a way to go and walked briskly on.

Was I quite without fear? I think I was.

How dead I was and yet how driven. Then all at once I heard this sound ahead, like the chink of coins. I reached out my hands and felt his coat of mail. Tepid and damp! I plunged my fingers deep inside.

Did I say something? Or did he? I can't remember, but I do know that I suddenly understood.

They had all betrayed him – his father, who had left him and his little brother with the sultan and never come back; the sultan's son Mehmet, who had called himself his friend and then turned traitor; his little brother Radu, who had become an ardent Mussulman and fought with the Ottomans against his own flesh and blood ... Always the same poisonous ambition, the same thirst for money and power. But it made him strong. The more he was wronged, the stronger God made him. He battled tirelessly against this evil until the end of days.

Those around him knew neither honour nor faith in a higher justice – only greed and baseness. The boyars, the neighbouring princes, his liegemen, his kinsmen, the populace – they were a spineless lot, without exception, and it was up to him to give them a spine. The stake!

Even when his own men stabbed him in the back and, hypocrites that they were, picked him up and held him in their arms, he told them – with blood spewing from his mouth – that it was not over. By God, he would come back and fight this battle to the end.

We lay there – I on him, or he on me – and I asked whether I should have come in the green shoes, the ones that had belonged to his lover Ecaterina Fronius Siegel. He laughed that deep laugh of his, almost a roar, and I said, 'Come to thy lord and master, Ecaterina. There is a war out there, and I must go and fight.' I fingered his mail shirt and licked his fingers between his rings. 'Come to thy lord and master.' And pulling myself up, I grabbed his flaxen hair and kissed his face – the side of his nose, his bushy moustache, his mouth. I kissed the fleshy lips, the teeth, the lips again, biting until I drew blood.

We rolled about along the passage, an ever-narrowing passage lined with sandy earth that seemed to *flow*, and we bumped against the rough walls with dull thuds. I scraped against them and against his chainmail, chafing my shoulder blades and cheeks, my knees and hands, my breasts and belly, while all around us the air jangled as if it were raining coins.

'That's it!' I cried, pushing him away. 'That's it, my love! I must go!'

First crawling and then bolt upright, I made my way towards the pale light and out into the open.

The four guards were still there, and when they looked at me I recognised the awed gaze of warriors before their leader. I signalled to them and they followed me word-lessly down the hill, over fences, through scrub and tall grass and deserted farms, to the old Dacia where cold drinks and pretzels were sold during the day.

The Dacia burnt first, blazing brightly, coughing black smoke. Then the souvenir kiosk went up, licked by yellowish-red tongues of fire, the bottles inside shattering with white flashes.

The cranes crashed onto the construction workers' tool sheds, sending bursts of sparks into the sky, and the flames ate their way through the bushes to Sabin's black SUV which exploded in a huge ball of fire.

That night it was as bright as day in B.

People ran every which way, doubled over in the heat, clutching clothes to their mouths and noses. They filled zinc buckets and watering cans at the wells and threw water at the houses.

The fire swept through B. with a roar. I heard strange singing and realised it was the woodlark.

At the foot of the mountains, the town hall burnt along with the portable toilets outside. The fire briefly exposed the inside of the burning building and its clunky furniture before the beams collapsed with a hiss of embers.

Later Sabin arrived on the scene with his party cronies and Ata and – crawling along behind them – the small police car from the next town. By then, though, there was no stopping the fire. Only the inhabited houses had escaped the flames. With the help of Miss Sanda, the few peasants of B. and a handful of tourists, we had formed human chains to the wells.

No fire engine could come, because the roads were too narrow. No one had seen how the fire had broken out, but the police inspector immediately identified the cause: arson.

'It was arson,' I told the tourists as soon as I heard. And: 'There'll be a war!' It would be best, I said, if they left immediately.

XVII

Ex Ossibus Ultor

THE AFTERNOON WE WERE EXPECTING Mamargot back it rained for the third day in a row. The last of the grey ashes had been washed away in dark-grey rivulets and the smoke had largely dispersed and barely made our eyes itch any more.

Inside the house there was a smell of burnt aubergine skins, toast and pickled peppers – the simple fare that Mamargot liked to eat with champagne. The doors between the rooms stood wide open and all the lights were on – in the drawing room, the bedrooms, the boudoirs, the passages, the kitchen. Light merged into light, and for some inexplicable reason this made me sad.

I patrolled the house in a red velvet kimono to see that everything was in its place, checking the furniture, icons and rugs to make sure nothing had been moved. Then I heard the familiar groans and creaks of the worn parquet, and a crackling noise started up, right under my feet.

Adieu, notre petite table . . .

The aria seemed to come from very far away – it seemed to come from the horn gramophone that had belonged to Mamargot's father.

What was this? Who would have put a record on? I went and examined the gramophone; it was indeed playing. I picked up the sleeve that was lying next to it – a battered Hariclea Darclée recording that no one had played for a very long time.

Adieu, notre petite table,
Qui nous réunit si souvent!

The label on the record showed a yellowing picture of the 'Carpathian nightingale', Hariclea, with her big eyes. She was looking up with a smile, like someone swept away on a carousel, and her hands were gripping a table, spinning it round and round and round.

Adieu, notre petite table ... She sounded as if she were making fun of the goodbye, impatient to get it over with – and her face spun fast as she sang. It spun so fast that her bun threatened to come loose, but it managed to keep its shape.

All right then. It looked as if Mamargot was going to be greeted with music.

I raised the tonearm and placed the needle a few grooves further in, just before Hariclea's glorious aria 'Vissi d'arte, vissi d'amore'.

It was an aria that Mamargot and I had loved when I was a child. The lamenting Tosca was a favourite motif of mine; I had drawn countless pictures of her, bowed over, wringing her hands, distressed at the impotence of her art to change anything. I had also sketched the chief of police, Scarpia, who has Tosca's lover tortured and refuses to be softened by her aria.

> *I lived for art, I lived for love*
> ...
>
> *In this hour of grief,*
> *Why, why, o Lord,*
> *Why do you reward me thus?*

Actually, Mamargot would say, art was quite capable of saving the world. Only a blockhead like Scarpia could fail to be moved or changed by such an aria.

Hardly was I out of the room than I heard it again, louder this time. *Adieu, notre petite table...*

Someone had moved the arm.

I was back at the record player in a flash.

There was nobody there.

I raised the tonearm and brought it round to the middle of the record to turn the gramophone off, then returned the arm to its rest and secured it with the latch. It struck me as unusually heavy and unwieldy, and I couldn't shake the thought that it was a dead arm that I was moving in the sign of the cross over a dead body.

A horrible thought. I made the sign of the cross over myself.

Where are you, sinner? Show yourself.

I looked about me, scanning the room for movement.

I listened.

The noise was coming from outside, a steady crackle.

And from the kitchen the rapid clack of a knife against a chopping board.

A gust of wind blew a pattering of rain against the window.

But it wasn't that.

It was much closer.

All around me.

I felt it on my skin, a tweaking sensation – the restlessness of rigid things.

I became aware of a twitch in my eyes – or of something twitching in the room.

It was her!

Yes, it was her!

'Miss Sanda,' I called out shrilly. 'Come here, please!'

'Coming,' she called. 'Coming.'

She was holding a checked teacloth in her hands and smelt of garlic.

'Did you put the music on?'

'No,' she said. 'Why?'

'The record player was on.'

Miss Sanda stared at me.

'I've never touched that record player in my life.'

'Well, that's all right, then,' I said. 'Shall I put something on for us? Anything particular you'd like to hear?'

She shrugged. 'Whatever *you* want to hear.'

'Don't you care?'

'It isn't that I don't care,' she said. 'I want to hear what *you* want to hear.'

I had the impression that she sounded different from usual – but perhaps I'd never really listened to her before.

'It's all right,' I said, putting Hariclea Darclée on the stack with the other records. 'I don't want to hear anything just now.'

Miss Sanda shrugged again and returned to the kitchen. I stayed in the drawing room, watching her go.

But a moment later – I had wandered only as far as the piano – the aria started up again. *Adieu, notre petite table* ... And in the same instant, I saw something else. I called Miss Sanda back and she came out of the kitchen door holding the same checked teacloth.

'Was that you?'

I pointed at the poppies in the vase. Had she put those poppies on the piano?

'Well, yes,' she said. 'Who else?'

They had been placed directly in front of my painting of a vase of poppies, making the picture look like a mirror.

'Do you like it?' she asked sharply.

I didn't reply.

We stood there for a long time in front of those two vases of poppies, the music surging over us with an unmistakably mocking tone. *Adieu! Adieu! Adieu!*

I didn't stir, waiting for Miss Sanda to make the first move. But she stood as still as I did, looking in the same direction.

'Yes,' I said eventually. 'It's good.'

Slowly she turned and fixed me with her eyes. And for the first time ever I saw her smile – a smile that distorted her entire face.

'I knew it,' she said.

I held her gaze and smiled too.

'All right then,' I said. 'Down we go.'

We climbed down the stairs – those stairs I knew so well – and I clung to the banister, the way I always did.

I'd heard the cars long before they turned off onto our road. Now the headlamps were shining at us through the fence.

I held the umbrella over Miss Sanda's head as she opened the garden gates. There they were: Mamargot with Yunus, Geo and Ninel with the Tudorans.

'Back in Paradise, at last,' cried Mamargot, who was the first to hug me.

I looked at her face: her eye was healed.

'At last, Mamargot! At last you're back!'

I got hugs from them all, including Yunus, whose pungent green-apple and vetiver aftershave clung to me. Then, as if compelled by some mysterious force to repeat the old words, I heard myself say, 'We've missed you. I thought you'd forgotten us.'

'No, no,' cried Mamargot, letting someone take her coat. 'How could he forget us?'

Yunus clasped my hands and smiled contentedly from under his antediluvian black fringe.

'Glass of water, Johnny?' I asked.

'Let him take his coat off first.'

The guests came charging in.

A cork popped in the kitchen and Mozart's 'Turkish March' was banged out on the piano.

Geo played with sweeping gestures and a lot of jiggling about. Whenever he reached a particularly rousing passage, Madame Tudoran gave a yelp of joy.

'I adore thunderstorms,' Mamargot cried.

'Me too!' cried Ninel.

'And me!' cried Madame Tudoran in a sharp voice.

'And me!' said Yunus, his eyes on mine.

Mamargot asked Miss Sanda to open the windows so that we could hear the rain, and to bring shawls so that we wouldn't be bothered by the draught at table.

'A superb kimono,' Mamargot said, before draping me in a shawl.

'Her noble pallor is most becoming,' cried Madame Tudoran in that sharp voice of hers.

'But she ought to get some sun,' Ninel opined. 'And eat more!'

'Ergo bibamus!' Geo shouted, and everyone laughed.

Miss Sanda went round with a tray of glasses.

'Prosit!' cried Madame Tudoran.

'Gaudeamus igitur!' Yunus cried, and everyone laughed again.

'Praesente medico nihil nocet,' Mamargot said, her eyes on Yunus – and the laughter swelled.

They drank and held out their glasses to be refilled – and the curtains billowed almost to the table and then fell again.

The aubergine salad was highly praised, and hands crisscrossed the table, reaching for the toast and the tomato salad with garlic, the pickled capsicums and the black pepper.

'Drink!' they urged me. 'Eat!'

And Geo came round with the red wine, shouting, 'In vino veritas!'

Even Mr Tudoran felt drawn to speak then. 'In hoc signo vinces,' he announced.

'Please,' his wife said, immediately disapproving. 'No blasphemy at table.'

'But that's not blasphemy...'

'Oh, come on!'

'In vino veritas!' Geo yelled again.

And Yunus countered with, 'Gaudeamus igitur!'

Then Geo tapped his spoon against his crystal glass, and when all was quiet he stood up and declaimed: 'Qui bibit, dormit; qui dormit, non peccat; qui non peccat, sanctus est!'

Madame Tudoran yelped with joy at this, and the others called out 'Yes!' and 'Too true!' and applauded loudly.

Mamargot looked at me, and Ninel must have noticed because she said, 'Qui tacet, consentire videtur!'

Everyone laughed and held out their glasses to be topped up again – and the thunder roared so loudly at the open window that not only the windows rattled, but the raised glasses too.

'Ex ossibus ultor,' I said, and all eyes turned to me.

'Ultor?' Geo asked.

'Mars Ultor!' Mr Tudoran explained. 'Iniuriarum!'

Everyone nodded, mystified.

'That's the way with these children of Communism,' Mr Tudoran said. 'Haven't read a thing, not even George Coşbuc!'

'Oh, come on,' his wife said.

'It's true,' said Geo. 'That's what we are – children of Communism.'

'Someone explain!' Ninel begged.

'Exoriare aliquis nostris ex ossibus ultor!' Mr Tudoran proclaimed.

'Ah!' Mamargot cried with delight. 'Dracula!'

'Bravo!' Madame Tudoran cried, clapping her hands.

And Geo sang George Coșbuc's poem about the harsh prince who was killed and buried. His killers cursed his memory and reverted to their wicked ways, but it was said that in stormy weather a white lightning bolt lit up the forgotten grave, and that, one day very soon, that grave would open.

Everyone laughed and raised their glasses.

'To Dracula!'

'To Dracula!'

Then they regaled me with a story that I, in my sequestered life, could not yet have heard and that they had avidly saved up for me – the final episode of the Dracula Park saga.

They told me about the latest revelations, what the newspapers were saying, what was being broadcast on television and who'd appeared on which chat shows – and the more they talked, the louder they got, laughing and interrupting one another, agreeing with Mamargot, making fun of each other.

The fires in B. had brought Dracula Park into the media. The government was accusing the opposition of literal arson. Not to be outdone, the opposition was accusing the government of literal *and figurative* arson: first they'd discredited the country's most heroic prince by turning him into a dime-novel cardboard cut-out, then they'd set up a Dracula PLC and misappropriated the money, and now they'd set fire to their own huts in order to report huge non-existent losses and claim yet more money on the insurance.

'Hear, hear!' yelped Madame Tudoran.

And her husband said, 'Auri sacra fames!'

They even wanted to cut down the local forest for their horror theme park; the Austrian firm Schweighofer was signed up for the job. Incredible that they were still here, those Austrians, after all those scandals and court cases!'

'Like vultures!'

'Like vampires!'

It was appalling, Mamargot agreed.

Over a quarter of Carpathian timber was illegally felled, and the court in Bucharest had at last established that Schweighofer was involved in illegal logging and timber trading. It had taken years of to-ing and fro-ing to reach this ruling – appeals from Greenpeace and the WWF, countless 'Save the Rainforest' campaigns, demonstrations on Bucharest's University Square, even repeated interventions on the part of Prince Charles who was a great fan of the Carpathians. But the Schweighofers had clearly had some expensive PR advisors and claimed to have done nothing illegal. It wasn't their fault, they told the media, if the politicians in Romania were corrupt, the laws wishy-washy and the people willing to chop down their own forests. Nor, to the best of their knowledge, had they ever seen a sign saying *National Park*.

'They have a point.'

'Don't talk nonsense, darling.'

'We've brought it all on ourselves.'

'Oh, come off it, they're crooks, the lot of them.'

Then came the revelation about Dracula Park and the kickbacks offered by the Schweighofers for the deforestation job.

At that point the Austrians had finally pulled in their horns – and moved their illegal clearing campaigns a little further north, into Ukraine.

Spineless, that's what they were!

'Too true!'

'They should be horsewhipped!' Geo said.

'The only way to deal with them,' Madame Tudoran agreed.

'Carpe noctem,' I said.

Madame Tudoran glared at me.

'Corruptio optimi pessima!' her husband said.

Madame Tudoran turned on him angrily.

'That's enough, darling.'

So now the plans for a Dracula theme park were definitively off the table. There would be no Dracula Park, not in B. or anywhere else.

I have a crystal-clear memory of the plate in front of me with its border of crossed gold swords. There were a hundred and sixty-four altogether. I counted them at a glance.

'So the plan's definitely off?' I asked with feigned breeziness.

That was correct, Madame Tudoran said. The plan for a Dracula theme park was definitively off the table.

Talk turned to vampires. It was agreed that vampires had no business in B.; they were a foreign invention, nothing to do with local tradition.

On the television show *Bucharest, the Day After*, Professor Irmicescu had talked about the origins of Bram Stoker's *Dracula*. Stoker's plan – this was in the late nineteenth century, soon after Victoria's coronation as Empress of India – was to write a horror story about a diabolical character from a distant foreign country who was hell-bent on destroying Britain. This fiend was to come from a dark forest and Stoker's original idea was to set his novel in the dark forests of Styria, in Austria. (At this point, apparently, the presenter had observed that this wouldn't have been far off the mark; the baddies really did come from Austria – just look at Schweighofer Timber Company, deforesting huge swathes of protected national parks in cahoots with the Romanian government.) But then Stoker met a Hungarian professor who introduced him to a book called *Cosmographia* by Renaissance scholar Sebastian Münzer. This cosmography was a compendium of the knowledge of the time; Münzer had asked for contributions to his book all over the world, in every country known to him. It was in this way that he became acquainted with the Transylvanian Saxons' slanderous pieces on Vlad the Impaler – horror stories about the Wallachian Prince and his protectionist trade policies. The Saxons in Wallachia were excluded from retail trade and permitted only to sell their wares wholesale at the border, and they were aggrieved that the prince refused all bribes and never swerved from his laws, but had them impaled immediately, however petty their crimes.

'Quite right too,' Madame Tudoran observed.

And Geo recited: 'Impaler, lord, wouldst thou but come / To rule with iron fist.'

So it was, then, that Stoker, a Protestant Irishman, came to hear about Vlad Dracula, and when he read that the Transylvanian Saxons had portrayed him as blood-thirsty, he got it into his head that Vlad had been Transylvanian – a high-ranking person, possibly a count – and that the dragon in his name was to do with his devilish nature: just the man for the hero of a horror story! In fact, all Prince Vlad had done was to insist upon justice, whatever the cost. 'Dura lex, sed lex!' How different from the chaos of today.

'Did they ever find out who killed Traian?' I asked.

'Killed whom?' Mamargot asked.

'The man on our grave.'

'No. But can anyone else hear this music coming from outside?'

Indeed they could, between the bursts of thunder.

They got up and went to the window and, quietened by the roaring storm, they peered out.

XVIII

Allah, Help Her

To the right of the entrance, in the pronaos, was a painting of Saint Mary of Egypt with dishevelled hair and a loose cloak worn open to reveal her emaciated breast. In her hand she held a scroll with the legend: *The kingdom of God is not meat and drink; but righteousness, and peace, and joy in the Holy Ghost.* I stopped and made a big sign of the cross, from forehead to navel and from right shoulder to left.

Mary the Egyptian, the story goes, was prevented by an unseen force from entering a church in Jerusalem. It was only after praying and vowing to renounce her harlot's life and go wherever God might send her, that she was able to go in and see the cross.

No such force held me back, and I stepped into our little church with a nice sense of confirmation – *I* had succumbed from the start to the force that had *me* in its grip.

The sweet scent of incense wafted towards me and a piped Byzantine chorale came from the chancel. I crossed myself again and kissed the two-faced icon of Christ Pantocrator with Yunus beside me. He stood rather stiffly, but not, I am glad to say, with his hands in his pockets.

Ever since his arrival in B., he'd been following me like a shadow. Occasionally he would dispense medical advice – get out into the fresh air, eat more vitamins, you're rather pale, there's a feverish look in your eyes. I tolerated his company, not sure that it wasn't Mamargot who had put him up to it.

This was a very beautiful church, he said. So beautifully painted – and these silver-framed icons, also very beautiful. He liked Romanian churches; they were unlike any others.

I signalled to him to be quiet, and entered the naos. And then it happened. I felt myself trembling violently all over, as if I were wobbling in and out of the contours of my body. Meanwhile, the cherubikon went on and on, torturously slow with long-drawn-out words. 'Let us lay aside all cares, all earthly cares.' I could see the sounds written in the air around me.

'But these martyrs,' I heard Yunus say from the pronaos. 'Does anyone ever look at them?'

Beheaded, drowned, stabbed to death, chopped to pieces, burnt at the stake, buried alive.

'Have you seen them?' he asked. 'Look.'

Vivid scenes of carnage, so prettily rendered.

Victims and executioners alike beautifully dressed, in red and blue and gold.

What magnificent colours!

'And those jets of blood!' Yunus said, and laughed.

But his laugh was short-lived, because I crept up behind him and whispered in his ear, making him jump. 'Well spotted,' I said. 'The martyrs and executioners are all as well-dressed as each other.'

If he looked closely, I added, he would see that most of the martyrs were on all fours, like animals.

And look, those round haloes made their heads look like rolling balls.

'Creepy,' he said with frank horror and reached for my hand.

Such images could scare even a doctor.

Luckily for him he was in the company of an intrepid woman.

My hand slipped from his clasp like smoke, and I found myself standing in front of the racks of candles: the rack for the living on the left, the rack for the dead on the right, and in between, a bucket for the candle stumps.

'I thought you were still next to me,' Yunus said when he caught up with me. 'Shall we light a candle?'

The trembling had quite stopped now. I was compact, filled with my power. I could have wheeled round to Yunus, my arm outstretched, commanding.

Silence, I wanted to say, but the first notes of the Kyrie sounded from the chancel and I was silent myself.

When I did turn to Yunus, it was with the calm of one who holds back his power in favour of serene humility.

'Forgive me. I'll show you everything.'

What power I felt now that I had no need to demonstrate my power.

As he stood there beside me, I could feel the warmth of his skin and hear the dull murmur of blood in his veins. Through the pungent scent of his green-apple aftershave, I even caught the faintly rancid whiff of sweat.

I resisted it all – indeed, I felt horror at the very idea that resistance might not be easy.

'The kingdom of God is not meat and drink; but righteousness, and peace, and joy in the Holy Ghost.'

There he was, hovering close, with his vacuous face and dull doe-like eyes and that antediluvian black fringe.

I explained all the frescoes in the pronaos to him and told him the stories of the martyrs. I told him about Saint Stephen who was stoned, about Cyrus and John the doctor saints, devout Cornelius the Centurion, Saint Philothea who was killed with an axe, the holy fathers slain at Sinai and Raithu, and the forty martyrs of Sebaste whose bones were crushed with hammers, but who gladly suffered execution for their faith.

Yunus interrupted me with a strained attempt at flippancy, declaring his approval of the Wallachian feast for the martyrs of Sebaste – little glazed rings with cinnamon and walnut. So much better than the Moldovan feast which was only dry bread and honey with a few crumbs of crushed nuts.

Anyone could see he was weak, I said. Even imagining the martyrs' torments was too much for him, so he distracted attention by being facetious.

He shrugged his shoulders and said he didn't like gratuitous violence, that was all.

Indeed, I said, we were creatures of comfort. But the holy martyrs had looked hell in the face. Unflinchingly, I said. They had set an example of steadfastness that was sorely lacking in this country – and indeed in most other places.

'Aren't I steadfast?' Yunus asked.

The sounds around me began to grow louder – even the sound of the carpet loops bristling under Yunus's feet.

Did I believe in saints, Yunus asked. Did I believe they never rotted.

My gaze came to rest on the icon of the death of the Virgin, but I couldn't see myself in the glass – only Yunus with his dull eyes staring into space.

I made another sweeping sign of the cross.

It was rare now, I said, for people to give themselves unflinchingly to pain and suffering, but there used to be many who displayed such fortitude and strength of faith – and did so with reverence. These days there was no reverence – only scorn and flippancy.

I heard someone come in and switch on the chandelier. A woman in a headscarf shuffled past us in plastic mules and prostrated herself in front of the icon of the Mother of God with a great deal of sighing and moaning.

The painters of these icons are said to have fasted and prayed while they were painting. These days, the restorers come to work with their phones and their ham sandwiches – and out in the churchyard, the mayor dispenses free wine and hands out campaign flyers. Well, and what if he does ... He's a nice old man, everyone knows him – all right, so he steals the funds that come from Bucharest, but he's hardly the first. And so the locals vote for him year in year out, and when the time's ripe they vote for his son. Both from round here. Homegrown guys who speak the language of these poor wretches – the language of defiance, of persisting in sin!

Why bother trying to escape from this miserable life just because of what a few city folk say who come here on holiday? Why be in awe of people just because they've learnt more and so supposedly know more?

These poor wretches, they defy knowledge, they defy all power and they claim that power as their own.

Let the world go to hell!

The woman in the headscarf paused for a moment, then went back to prostrating herself with even louder sighs.

Yunus laughed.

That laugh!

I blinked and blinked and breathed faster, but the laughter went on, obstinately refusing to do as it was told.

Then the young priest came in. I blinked him past us so quickly that he almost flew, and the woman in the headscarf twittered, 'I kiss your hand, Father.'

'My wife cooks so well on fasting days,' the priest called out to us, 'I sometimes wonder if it counts as fasting ...'

He was in a good mood.

Had I brought the young man to church to make an Orthodox Christian out of him, he asked teasingly.

Yunus laughed.

The priest shook his hand and asked his name, then invited us to sit down on the stools along the wall.

Yunus?

Excellent! *Yunus* came from Jonah, one of his favourite books in the Tanakh.

I found myself trembling again and leaned sideways against the cold wall with all the saints – they stood bolt upright and so close together that their haloes overlapped. Behind the saints were more saints, and behind those, yet more, only their haloes visible. My trembling spread to the colours I was leaning against, swirling them round as if the wall were made of water. But no one seemed to notice anything; the priest talked and talked, telling the story of the prophet Jonah.

Jonah was sent by God to the sinful city of Nineveh to warn the people there that they would bring down God's judgment on themselves if they persisted in their wickedness. But Jonah didn't want to go to Nineveh. He knew that God is a graceful and merciful God who would not enforce his judgment against the city – and he, Jonah, was a harsh prophet who believed in the castigation of the sinful. Why should he go to Nineveh and threaten the people there with God's punishment just so that the sinners could repent and be shown mercy?

So he didn't go to Nineveh, but set off in the opposite direction, to Joppa, and there he caught a ship to Tarshish. But at sea there was a mighty storm and when the ship looked as though it might sink, Jonah confessed to the sailors that God's wrath was meant for him; if they wanted to calm the sea and save themselves, they must throw him overboard. And when they threw Jonah into the sea he was swallowed by a whale, and he was in the dark belly of that whale for three days and three nights, just as Christ would be three days in the realm of the dead.

How long are three days? I should have asked. How long does the darkness last?

But what use would an answer have been to me?

The priest told us with great spirit of how God had taught Jonah the importance of humility over pride. His finger shot up; he spoke rousingly. 'Don't forget: humility, not pride! Humility and love!'

With a name like his, Yunus said, he should almost get himself christened, shouldn't he?

But now that he was in church with a priest, he'd like to make a confession: he used to be an atheist – because of his communist leanings. The priest sighed and looked up to heaven, or perhaps he rolled his eyes. It was different in Iraq, Yunus said. Communism had been kind of punk there – something for savvy young people with more spirit than the rest.

He'd had a Jewish mother who had put a great deal of imagination into concealing her faith from her Iraqi neighbours. At Ramadan, she lit the lamps in the house before dawn so that the neighbours would think they were eating. After sunset, when people broke their fast, she did the same. And although other women in their town wore jeans and showed their hair, she always went out in a headscarf.

When she was dying and the Muslim neighbours were watching at her bedside to say the shahada with her – 'I bear witness that there is no god but Allah, and I bear witness that Mohammad is the servant and messenger of Allah' – his mother sat up in bed and cried, 'It's time you knew. I'm Jewish!'

For a moment there was silence. Nobody spoke, not even her husband or children. No one dared move, unsure what the truth would unleash – until one woman burst out sobbing and cried, 'She's mad! Our dear sister has gone mad!'

And soon they all had tears running down their faces and, raising their arms to heaven, they cried out, 'Allah, help her!'

When the time came, they helped my mother to say the last prayer by whispering the words into her ear: 'I bear witness that there is no god but Allah, and I bear witness that Mohammad is the servant and messenger of Allah.'

Yunus looked the priest in the eyes. The priest looked at me.

XIX

The Body in the Forest

ON SOME NIGHTS, THAT PIERCING scream was heard again. Mamargot and our guests would say the next morning that it had woken them – that they had looked out to see what it was. Could they have dreamed – a collective dream?

From the roof of our house I saw the peasants looking out of their windows too. But nobody went out.

Maybe it wasn't a scream at all. Maybe it was some kind of echo from the mountains.

One afternoon – we were having tea in the garden – Miss Sanda came running up with a tray, and tripped and fell. She let out a sharp cry, and the sliced cozonac went sailing over our heads into the lilacs.

She must, she said, tell Mamargot about the mushroom pickers and the dead woman.

'Oh, please don't,' said Ninel.

But Madame Tudoran said briskly, 'Please tell us everything. Our sort have been through a thing or two. We're braced, aren't we, Margot?'

'Sit down with us, my trusty one,' Mamargot said. 'What's happened now?'

And so Miss Sanda sat down at the garden table and told us all about the mushroom pickers and the dead woman who had disappeared. She went into great detail, as people here did, and she kept saying 'well'.

The mushroom pickers, it seemed, had gone into the forest the day before – not down towards the old weaving mill, but up to the right, towards Ata's house, where the best porcini grew. There were tall spruces and beeches up that way, and the ground was covered in a thick layer of russet leaves. Old Simion, who danced the goat dance and was a bit of a prankster, had pushed old Camelia – she of the magenta hair – onto a big pile of leaves. And old Camelia had started to scream like a stuck pig, because next to her in the leaves was a dead woman!

A dead woman who looked familiar to everyone.

The men doffed their caps. If only they'd had a candle with them – the woman didn't look as if she'd been dead long. They'd never seen such a beautiful corpse, the skin firm and gleaming like porcelain, the breasts bared, the nipples still pointed and rosy. The only blemish was at the side of the woman's neck, where the skin was puckered as if from a deep bite. Maybe she had bites in other places too, but it was impossible to tell because of the leaves, and because of the cloak she was wearing. She had this black cloak draped over her arms, which presumably, beneath the leaves, also covered her from the waist down.

Someone had the idea of ringing at the young mayor's door – his house was just across the way.

But the old folk didn't dare – not even Simion, who was the goat every year and should have dared more than most.

So they went away.

By then it was about nine or ten in the morning.

One of them said they should go and get the priest, but Simion said no, first they should go up Internet Hill and see if there was anything on the news, and then they should ring the police in the next town. Old Camelia with the magenta hair disagreed. She said first they should fetch the old mayor – they didn't want things to turn against them.

Neither was prepared to give way and neither felt like accompanying the other, so no one went anywhere and they all spent the rest of the day at home.

But that evening they came together again and there were others there too. And when the others heard what they'd found in the forest, they got curious and wanted to see the beautiful corpse for themselves.

And so they all trooped off to the forest, up to the right, towards Ata's house where they'd foraged for porcini that morning, and they looked for the mound of leaves under the tall spruces and beeches.

They found a great deal of leaves which they tossed in the air, timidly at first, then boldly, wildly. But the dead woman was nowhere to be found.

This caused resentment towards the mushroom pickers. People jeered at them and mocked them. There'd never been anything there, they said – the mushroom pickers had made it all up so they'd have something to boast about. As if anything ever happened here. It was different in Spain and Italy where their children lived: there were real gangs there and secret societies – and the mafia, who were very bold in their methods.

On the way back, when they were almost out of the forest, one of them thought he saw something big in a tree. But no one dared look up; they were all too scared.

By morning, Miss Sanda said, news of the woman had reached the priest, and he, too, set off into the forest with his deacon and two boys from the next town. Sabin had also heard the story and gone along to the scene with a big escort and the police from the next town – and Ata had shown up too, very concerned that a crime had been committed so close to his house. But none of them found the beautiful corpse. And although no one liked to admit it to the priest – because he always got upset and told them not to be superstitious – the general feeling was that the beautiful woman with the pale skin and the rosy nipples hadn't been dead in the usual way of dead people, but had got up from that bed of leaves all by herself. Hadn't she been seen up a tree? And didn't they hear her terrible scream at night? Now, at last, they knew who was killing the animals in the sheds, biting their necks and sucking their blood. A woman who appears in folklore as a bat, a spider dangling on a thread, a wolf or even a mysterious haystack.

The beautiful woman who seemed so familiar to everyone was one of the living dead.

Sabin, Miss Sanda said, had promised to look into the matter with the help of the police and the party. Also, he was talking of Dracula Park again.

'Isn't that just like him!' Mamargot shouted. 'He never gives up!' And ruefully she cried, 'Impaler, Lord, wouldst thou but come / To rule with iron fist.'

XX

Portrait of the Inexorable
Prince Vlad the Impaler

BOLT UPRIGHT, HEAD HELD HIGH, he stared at the copper curtain rail, his right leg extended, his left leg tucked under the velvet stool. He was posing for a portrait by that illustrious artist who had painted a number of other aristocrats at the Hungarian court – among them, of course, Ilona Szilágyi, King Matthias Corvinus's beautiful cousin, to whom there were plans to marry him.

He had dressed up for the portrait in the garb of the Wallachian prince he no longer was.

It was sweltering in the room; red-hot light came in through the closed curtains. He was wearing the red velvet coat with the broad sable collar and the heavy velvet cap with the rows of pearls and the cocked heron's feather.

Whatever he did, he mustn't move; he didn't want to blur the artist's lines. And so he kept still – or as still as he could – gazing into the distance at the curtain rail, silently counting his years of imprisonment at the

Hungarian court. He counted slowly. He counted the months and the seasons, and he tried to miscount so that he could start all over again, sitting motionless, with the heavy velvet cap on his head. He counted by the Gregorian calendar and he counted by the Julian calendar, with a leap day every four years. Then he counted his years with the Ottomans, adding them to his Hungarian years and weighing them up against his years of freedom.

But could you call that freedom? Was a man who fought for freedom free?

No! Never had he been free. All his life he'd been driven by a sense of duty, sweating it out in heavy armour, his skin itching, a host of fickle soldiers at his back.

He could only hope he'd be blessed with enough years to outlive them all – the king and the sultan and his impious brother Radu the Handsome who had ousted him from the throne. And those grasping Wallachian boyars – yea, every man jack of them, unto the seventh generation. Then, perhaps, far from those vile people, he would find his freedom and his peace.

'Doth the light vex ye?' the artist asked.

'No, begging your pardon,' said Dracula the Unstirring, blinking away his tears.

He tried to think of Countess Szilágyi – perhaps he could make the thought a pleasant one. If nothing else, it would stir up the quiet of his life.

How many years would this Hungarian countess add to his tally? There was no escape.

At first he had staunchly resisted marriage.

He had a war to wage, he'd told the king. He must get back on his forebears' throne and fight. He must be cold-blooded if he wanted to fight for justice! The land of his fathers was going to rack and ruin.

How could he possibly marry again? A man whose wife had killed herself as they fled together, because she was too slow and didn't want to hold him up?

A warrior must live alone, like a monk. Like Saint George! Just him and his horse, the lance thrust deep into the dragon's throat.

But King Matthias Corvinus had laughed.

Saint George, he said, had battled against the dragon inside him. Dracula was far more of this world than the saint.

Didn't people say he was in love with the Transylvanian merchant's daughter, Ecaterina Fronius Siegel?

In love? Did he say *in love?*

Was that what the Transylvanian Saxons had put about in their stupid pamphlets? That and their slanderous claims that he impaled mothers and their sucking babes? Were those pamphlets in circulation at the Hungarian court – those libellous pamphlets that were rolling off the German printing presses instead of prayer books?

When that press was invented, people said it would make for justice. The printed word was to be for everyone, educated or no – it was to free them and empower them. But for what? Just look what the common people read when given half the chance. Lies and libel.

But he hadn't yet answered his question, the king said. Had he lived with this Ecaterina Siegel?

Lived? Now it was Dracula's turn to laugh.

Matthias had laughed too.

So there was nothing to prevent him from marrying the Countess Szilágyi or from entering into an alliance with his family, the royal family of Hungary?

Well, yes, there was something. He was a warrior, a loner.

Even a warrior needed offspring!

But he was a warrior, not a king. His offspring were all those who believed in justice, from generation to generation.

Be that as it may, Matthias had said. It was the king of Hungary's most heartfelt wish that he, Dracula, should marry the virtuous Countess Szilágyi here at the court. To refuse would be an unchivalrous slur – upon the famously fair and chaste Countess, and upon him, the king! Prince Vlad should think it over.

So he did. And he came to the conclusion that he had no choice. He must admit defeat.

'Countess Ilona Szilágyi has arched eyebrows just like Your Highness,' the artist said.

Dracula stopped staring at the copper curtain rail.

He was being kept prisoner here.

But why?

What charges did they bring against him?

The question had been tormenting him for years.

He was buried alive, knocking helplessly on the lid of his coffin.

Why was he being kept here? Why?

How could they doubt his steadfastness? How could they doubt the morals of Vlad Dracula, a worthy Athleta Christi!

Again he counted the years, trying to find a gap he'd overlooked.

The king was insistent that he marry here at the court. He needed the alliance as a guarantee of the prince's trust-worthiness. Maybe afterwards they would let him go ...

And again he fell to thinking of the many, many years, of his stagnant life and of Countess Szilágyi, with whom he was but fleetingly acquainted – when all at once it grew loud in the courtyard: hooves clattered, orders were yelled, maids screamed. Boots thumped on the wooden stairs; the air rang with shouts.

'Halt, you blackguard!'

Floors were trampled, furniture overturned, doors slammed.

Dracula doffed his velvet cap, took the big sword from the wall and left the room.

Out in the courtyard, his thundering voice asked, 'What are you doing in my house?'

The captain explained that they were hunting a runaway thief who was hiding there.

'Was I informed of this intrusion?'

There had not, he was told, been time.

'Well then,' said Dracula.

A blow fell.

There was a gurgle.

A rattle.

And the German artist, looking out of the window, saw his sitter Vlad Dracula with one foot on the headless torso of the Hungarian captain, one hand clutching the sword, the other dangling the pale head by its hair.

'This is my house and I am prince here,' he proclaimed solemnly to the terrified people in the courtyard. 'No one has the right to enter my house uninvited. And if a man seeks refuge here who is said to be a thief, I alone will judge that man and decide whether he deserves mercy – or punishment!'

XXI

Ata's Execution

FROM THE EDGE OF THE ROOF I could see my bedroom curtains billowing out of the window. I heard the rings rattle on the curtain rail – then someone screamed again.

That scream!

A piercing scream that had nothing human about it.

It was coming from the forest.

I took off and glided over the dark trees. The forest was still again – there was only the rustle of the treetops, the rushing of the river by the mill and, far away, the repeated call of a night bird. Everything green was now dark blue: the upward-reaching branches, the leaves, the backdrop of shimmering rock. I lowered myself like a spider on a thread, arms and legs splayed, and scuttled over the damp beech leaves to the small clearing outside Ata's house.

Then I straightened up, curious to meet the beautiful woman who was said to be a vampire.

There was a smell of moss and mouldy leaves.

Would she be well-disposed towards me?

Maybe she would, maybe she wouldn't.

But I was keen to be polite.

'Good evening,' I whispered. 'Are you there?'

There was no reply.

I was curious to see her all got up in that black cloak. For my part, I was wearing a white nightdress and tennis shoes: it would be a meeting of white and black.

I heard something jump over Ata's fence – several things. They ran from me through the leaves, whimpering. I smelt their doggy spittle and their tallowy coats.

Should I go after them? But what would be the point?

I rang Ata's doorbell.

Why I did that is a mystery to me. Afterwards I came up with all kinds of explanations, but although many of them seemed plausible enough, the reverse always seemed equally true.

Time passed. Then Ata's nasal voice came over the intercom.

'It's me,' I said. 'Will you let me in?'

He came down and opened the gate himself.

I was alone? In that get-up? He couldn't believe I'd dared – through the forest at night – to visit him.

He led me across the courtyard, and that was when I first felt it – a kind of warning. A tingling scalp, slight dizziness and a pronounced feeling of disgust – a dry tickle in my mouth as if I'd eaten too much garlic. A flash of premonition in the midst of my stupor; I felt myself slipping on the grey pebbles.

Grey pebbles!

Yes, those pebbles were the only false note. Apart from them, it was the same path with the same unnecessary bends. In our garden, the pebbles were white.

It was then that I realised the awful truth. Everything – flowers, hedges, lilacs, benches – was the same as in our garden. Only slightly different, like something in a dream. The house, too, was exactly the same: a misshapen building with a balcony running the length of the first floor, and painted white so that it seemed to shimmer in the moonlight, the shadows of the surrounding trees patterning the walls as the branches blew this way and that in the wind. Beneath the balcony a small sign was engraved with the words *Villa Diana*.

I shuddered at the thought of going in and finding the same furniture as in our house, only slightly disarranged – or, worse still, the old furniture that I'd seen in our cellar.

Was I scared of his dogs, Ata asked. I didn't need to be scared when he was there.

First I'd like to see the tennis courts, I said. He had tennis courts, didn't he?

Of course, he said. Two courts, like Mrs Margot. Would I like to play a match with him, by floodlight? Or would I rather see inside the house first? He came very close as he said that. I felt his breath on my neck.

I'd love a game of tennis, I said. If he was man enough to take me on.

The floodlights flickered and came on – a pale light, like at full moon.

The white plastic markings shone luridly.

The clay court was blue rather than red. A friend of Sabin had got hold of the clay for Ata – a former tennis player and successful businessman who often came to the area to hunt.

You could see the ball much better on blue clay, Ata said, as we knocked a few balls back and forth. In Madrid they'd said the surface was more slippery than red clay and the ball didn't bounce as high, but it wasn't true.

The blue clay made it look like a hard court, I said. You expected concrete – that was why you slipped, and why you were surprised when the ball didn't bounce higher. A kind of illusion!

Ata laughed. 'If you say so!'

The racquet Ata had lent me sat as nicely in my hand as my own: the same head size, the same string gauge, the same weight – a weight that vanished when I swung it, as if the racquet were an extension of my arm.

When had I last played?

It was like hearing forgotten heartbeats – *plop* – *plop*, *plop* – *plop* – like remembering a distant life.

A breeze swept past with the rushing sound of all passing things, and my hair fluttered on my forehead. I felt strangely moved at the sight of the returning ball which I reached just in time to lob it back into my opponent's court.

The satisfying *plop* on my racquet echoed off the surrounding tree trunks before the green ball was returned to me – *plop!*

And again the ball rose from my swinging arm. My racquet whistled through the air and – *plop!*

And back again – *plop!*
A one-handed backhand – *plop!*
And back again – *plop!*
A nifty squat shot – *plop!*
And back again – *plop!*
A long-line hit – *plop!*
And back again – *plop!* – and *plop!* I volleyed the ball and hit Ata's legs.

Ata said he couldn't concentrate. An opponent in a nightie – it was a bit distracting.

We walked to the net, collecting the balls, and when we met, Ata grabbed the back of my head and pressed me against his face and his swollen tongue. I let it happen. Racquet in hand, he stroked my back down towards my bum – until a branch cracked so loudly that he jumped back in fright.

It was only a branch, I said. What did he expect, living in a forest? Was he scared of the beautiful woman at his gate?

What woman, he asked. There was no woman. The only beautiful woman in the forest was standing in front of him in her nightie. How about a match now? Was I up for it?

You bet, I said and ran back to the service line.

I served first. I hit the ball low over the net to the centre line, then waited at the net and let Ata's return drop down.

'Serve-and-volley,' I said. 'Bang bang.'

'Fifteen–love,' Ata yelled.

I aced my next serve. Just like old times!

Then I hit a ball close to the sideline, and Ata misjudged and didn't even try to return it.

The next ball he dumped in the net.

'Game!' he said, and there was no mistaking his annoyance.

He claimed there was something the matter with his racquet and went to get a new one.

I secured the first set without too much swagger.

Did I let slip snide remarks when I won? Did I make involuntary gestures of scorn? I don't think so. I wouldn't want to speak ill of Ata – and anyway, *de mortuis nihil nisi bene* – but I must say he was a dreadful loser, and you could hardly call him a serious player. I had to listen to repeated complaints about my nightie, and when I jokingly referred to it as my 'tennis whites' he got furious. He was playing for victory, and I didn't let him win. He stood at the baseline, grimly returning ball after ball, until he slipped up again and hit another forehand out of bounds.

Whenever that happened, he would hurl his racquet to the ground, pick it up again and resume playing with some hefty wallops and not a hint of imagination.

Was I, you will ask, playing with greater power than usual. Did I fly to meet the ball, as in my childhood dreams? No! Absolutely not. I may have had those new powers, but I didn't use them; I was determined to play fair. It's true that I didn't get out of breath, but that would hardly have been a problem anyway, because Ata always hit the ball straight ahead – with force, but without tactics.

He didn't send me running from one corner to the other, up to the net and back to the baseline, the way I did with him. I think he was handicapped by his own ambition. And I didn't have to put too much power into my returns, because the power was all in the momentum of the half-pirouettes I turned as I hit the ball.

I was like a dancer, sidestepping, yielding to the rhythm of the ball, hitting it again and again with my favourite one-handed backhand, my right toes dragging over the sand.

I even managed to flick a backhand with my back to the court.

'You're playing well,' I called out encouragingly to Ata – the way you do in a friendly game.

I took the ball at the net, forcing him back behind the baseline, where he caught the ball but then skidded and missed my teasing dropshot.

Again he hurled his racquet to the ground.

'Quiet, please,' I called in my best Wimbledon English. He raised his hands apologetically, but didn't smile.

With the next ball, I lured him up to the net and played a high lob that landed on the court behind him.

'Wouldn't have happened on red clay,' I quipped.

After that he dumped several balls in the net.

And so the game descended from what Mamargot would have called a 'dialogue of balls' to a simple mono-logue. I smashed the ball; Ata was caught off guard and failed to return it.

It was dreary. Like playing against a ball machine.

I called out that I was tired, and broke off the game.

Did I use to play with Traian like that too?
With Traian?

Yes, Traian.

I played other games with him, I said, returning his blow.

Yes, indeed, the little scumbag had made sure the whole of B. knew about *that*.

He had every right to.

I should have seen him, Ata said, standing at that gate there begging for work. Yes, Traian had come begging for work – any work – didn't matter what. Came back from Spain all bent and thin and hid himself away in his parents' empty house. Didn't want anyone knowing he was back. Because he was ashamed.

And then?

Oh yes, what wouldn't I give to know that!

Didn't he need anything?

He did not.

Did he give Traian work?

Of course he did. He got him to mow the grass in the clearing and on the hill. And he paid him for it. Traian spread the grass out to dry, then gathered it in and piled it into stacks before the rain came. And all the time he made sure no one saw him.

He'd come to Ata with a map: Look, here are your haystacks – ten here, fifteen there – what do you want me to do with them? And Ata had paid him for every last one – he never saw them, but he paid for them all. Then he said, Here's some more money, now go and burn that hay, burn the lot of it.

Traian completely lost it when he heard that – why would he burn all that hard work? What do you think, idiot, because it's no bloody use. Do you see any animals here?

So Traian took the money and set fire to the hay. Like the idiot that he was.

And then?

Then Traian's wife appeared in the forest. Stood screaming at his gate, saying he'd killed Traian. Why would he have killed him, Ata asked. But she stuck to her story: he had her husband on his conscience, it was his fault that she'd been left without a man – that she was a widow like her mother. She refused to take money and screamed until late into the night, and in the morning she came back, so he set the dogs on her. After that she stayed away.

'The woman was right,' I said. He and his father had destroyed everything here and chased everyone away.

Him? What had *he* done wrong?

He'd carried on doing everything his father had done wrong. He'd robbed the people.

He hadn't done anything.

He'd refused to make changes, he'd bowed to the injustice of the status quo. He looked down on the people he ought to be looking after, he lived the high life here, cut off from everyone.

He lived just like I did!

Wasn't he haunted by nightmares? Wasn't he afraid he'd be punished for the robbery, for all the misery in B.?

No, he yelled, he wasn't haunted by anything. And he wasn't afraid either. Who could hurt him?

On the pebble path, he tugged at my nightdress, so that it ripped at the shoulder. I kept going all the same. He made several grabs for me, but missed every time.

225

He whistled for his dogs, but they didn't come.

Was he beginning to feel scared?

I went on without looking back.

At the gate, something hit me on the shoulder – a tennis ball, or perhaps a stone. I think it startled him – his act of aggression, but more still, its lack of impact.

I walked on as if nothing had happened, and without saying goodbye.

Had I dreamt it all? And what about what happened next? Did I dream that?

I advanced through strips of red light, following the piercing scream. Far ahead I saw the red strips of that same scream fluttering high in the air. When I got there, I saw him up on the stake, his shirt torn.

Between the slats of the fence I saw the dark figure holding him by his splayed legs.

She pulled him down to her with a jerk, and the tip of the stake shot out between shoulder and head. It shone blue in the pale-red moonlight – and lapis blue wherever it was red.

XXII

The Ghost on the Path

I WALKED STEADILY, MATCHING my pace to my breathing, mesmerised by the rustle of leaves as I brushed past them. I saw the crosses for the hikers who had come to grief on the steep slope; I read once again the words *Travel well, stranger. My journey ends here.*

The damp leaves gleamed and, beyond them, the black cloak sailed up the hillside. I followed it – where? I think by then I already knew.

The pounding river grew louder, its many-voiced roar echoing in the gorge that lay before me, hung with long drifts of white mist. Here I was again, back on the same steep path where we'd had to wedge our feet between the jutting roots to find a foothold. I no longer had to do that. I was nimble and fearless.

I followed the black figure; I could have done it with my eyes closed – her presence was palpable to me. Was I already one of her kind?

I saw her through the milky mist, only a few paces ahead of me, the black cloak clinging damply to her slim body as she walked. Then she stopped, exactly where Madame Didina had stood before she fell. I was, it seems, to believe in fate.

The images flew at me fast and furious – images of this narrow path, the path of the cursed. I saw the traitors coming along it one by one, leading their horses by the bridle, and I saw them being ambushed by the faithful: man and horse, man and horse – one after another they plummeted to their deaths, a never-ending torrent. I looked away, but only for a moment. They had a barrel full of honey with them – and preserved in that honey for Sultan Mehmet II, Abu al-Fatih, was the body of Prince Vlad Dracula.

Ecaterina Fronius Siegel got down on her knees and mourned her lover who was laid out on cloths on the ground. Who had done this, she asked of the faithful, who stood about her, their heads bared. The traitors, her father said. Wallachians, Saxons, Hungarians, Ottomans and God knows who else. Powerful men and common folk who feared his authority – might they rot in darkness forever. The men crossed themselves, their gaze firmly on their hero. The prince's pale face gleamed beneath the honey lacquer, to which the insects of the forest were beginning to stick fast.

It grew quiet around us, the roar of the river no more than an unbearable raging silence. Here and there something crackled; space expanded and then contracted again.

Before me, the dark figure stood with her back to me, waiting. My fate! I stepped between the jutting roots towards the inevitable, noticing that although she stood stock-still, her hands were working their way out of the dark stuff of her cloak – long, pale fingers, curled like claws.

I stopped only half a pace from her.

Was that me, breathing like that?

Slowly, the creature turned around.

I was looking into the face of my friend Arina.

Her long face, her laughing eyes, the little bump on her nose just below the bridge.

She looked at me challengingly, like the night she'd climbed up the wall of our house.

There you are at last, I thought I heard her say. *My long-lost friend.* Her mouth didn't move. Only the familiar face twisted into a lascivious smile.

You lured me here, I replied with my eyes.

She raised a hand and spread her long claws. *I called you as one who calls her playmate.*

She moved languidly, as if she might pounce on me at any moment.

I looked fearlessly into her face. *Why did you kill Ata?*

Why? She began to laugh soundlessly, throwing back her head and shaking it to and fro. Her body, however, remained motionless, as if head and body were separate.

Tell me why.

When she looked at me again she was someone else – face furrowed, eyes wide, teeth bared – and I heard the words she had no need to speak out loud: *I came bearing Prince Vlad's stake, that cold spine for the spineless.*

Why? Would she yield to my patient gaze? *Why, Arina?*

She inclined her frightful face and came towards me, then moved away to one side again and I saw her cross the gorge on the drifts of mist.

Your friend Ata let my husband die and set his dogs on me.

He wasn't my friend.

Can't you just admit that you liked him?

Arina!

She was so familiar to me, and yet at the same time she was an ugly spectre walking on drifts of mist.

Did she hear at last the words I had never spoken for fear of hurting her feelings? *Your envy always stood between us, playmate mine. You thought me better off than you.*

She seemed very close in the white mist; I thought I heard her voice again.

A great deal separated us in life. But soon you will be like me – of the blood of Prince Vlad Dracula. Nothing will break us!

I noticed that my trainers were no longer touching the ground. Arina and I were hovering face-to-face, communing wordlessly.

The vampire's bite is not a punishment like the stake. It brings deliverance to the oppressed, the betrayed, the humiliated.

Yield up your weak blood! And then, o powerless ones who would lief be powerful, take and drink from the blood of the prince. This is the blood bond of those who fight for justice.

I was beginning to have trouble distinguishing my thoughts from Arina's.

I am an ever-living vampire of the blood of Prince Dracula. I am the eternal vengeance of the just.

XXIII

The Eternal Vengeance of the Just

'**M**AY I COME IN?'

'Yes,' he said, 'but how ...'

I don't know what scared him. It went very fast.

I hovered in a hunched position below Sabin's living-room ceiling, leaning down to the little man in pyjamas who was moaning incessantly, 'My leg, my leg!'

He'd wet himself and somehow got it into his head that he couldn't move the wet leg.

I ordered to him to be quiet with a loud 'Shhh', but it sounded more like the rattle of a snake than a call for silence. He went on moaning. 'My leg, my leg.'

There was a strong smell of ammonia – also of onions, schnapps and smoked sausage.

Sabin was lying with his back against the arm of the greyish-yellow leather sofa, kicking his feet.

It was a singularly ugly room; the view from above was excruciating. It was a room from the past, unchanged for decades, either because its owners couldn't be bothered, or because they liked things the way they were: the rug with the gory hunting scenes, the oil cloth and macramé on all the furniture, the little wicker baskets and the lacquered vases. Unopened parcels were piled up against two walls. I remembered coming into this room as a child, a bag of gifts in each hand – Sabin's invalid wife, who was in charge of letting the villas in B., had called out from the next room, 'Leave them on the sofa, poppet. I'll see what can be done.'

I gave the ugly ceiling lamp a kick, making it shatter. The light went out.

Down on the floor, I switched on the old standard lamp and we stood facing each other, both in dark coats.

'Your son Ata is dead,' I said.

Sabin nodded, his expression unchanged.

'My condolences.'

Again he nodded.

'Would you like a glass of water with sugar?'

He only stared at me – a puffy, sweaty face behind a bedraggled strand of hair.

Then, out of the blue, he asked, 'Was it you who set fire to my car?'

He didn't ask about his son.

'Was it you who killed Traian?' I asked in return.

'Traian?'

His eyes came to life. He smirked, then snorted with laughter. Colour shot into his face.

Then he told me about Traian.

He spoke with relish, quite forgetting that his pyjama trousers were wet, or that he was afraid of me, or that I'd brought news of his son's death. His scorn for the man he referred to as 'a poor wretch' allowed him to tell his story with peculiar gusto.

I'm not sure I can make you understand my aversion to Sabin. A spirited fellow with a finger in every pie, he's wheeled and dealed all his life, becoming such a presence in B. that he'd be missed if anything happened to him. He was boss here even during the dictatorship and was considered easy to get along with. A short while ago he installed his son as mayor – that arrogant guy who used his power to get rich, not like Sabin who's always mingled with the common folk.

People like him for that smug irony of his that passes for humour; everyone here is familiar with his derogatory way of talking about others. And yet, as he told me Traian's story, I began to see him as the source of all evil in B. – a man who cynically thwarted life.

He told me about Traian's wedding. There had, it seems, been an inappropriately lavish party, with musicians and dancing and a huge spread of food. Apparently, the bride's sister had sent money from Spain. Poor as church mice, they were – his family and hers. Poor as church mice, but extravagant with it. First thing they did after the wedding was to burn down the fence between the two farms and start to build themselves a house. They were all the same here – threw themselves into building without a plan, and no sooner was the cornerstone set than they realised they couldn't afford it. Then they'd come running to him: Mr Sabin, do you have a job for me? Mr Sabin, do you have a job for my wife? The way they carried on, you'd have thought he was the job centre in Bucharest.

Then Traian and his wife emigrated to Spain. They came back every summer with a load of money and continued the work on their house. Sabin had very kindly offered to oversee the construction work in their absence – they could have sent him money from Spain and he'd have seen to it that the house was built without too many interruptions. But Traian was suspicious and hadn't trusted him – as if Sabin had his eye on some puny return. In other countries, you blithering idiots, you have to apply for expensive planning permission; there's no nice mayor building your house for you for free. But what can you expect? They were fools, the pair of them.

Rather than save on travel costs and have the place built by pros, they'd preferred to do it themselves, and so Traian's wife had spent days on end listening to salsa music in the yard and mixing mortar while Traian hunted down cheap transport for his bricks. This went on summer after summer, until one year – like most people who moved away from B. – they stopped coming back. So many got burnt out working abroad; so many marriages broke down away from home. How could anyone make enough money to build a house in those conditions? And why bother anyway?

Most people who left as seasonal workers were never heard of again. Not so Traian: he made it big on the Spanish media – as a gullible idiot.

It all happened in a small town in northern Spain, where a hundred and twenty Romanians had gathered to celebrate a wedding. There was a live band all night long and dancing and only the best to eat and drink with no thought for the cost – and at the end of the night they finished off with the conga, snaking their way through the restaurant and the kitchen (where the staff cheered them on), round the lobby of the hotel next door, and in and out of the palm trees outside. It wasn't until head waiter Traian came out of the kitchen with the wedding cake topped with sparklers that he realised they'd done a runner! He was on the news the next day, saying all wide-eyed what a shock it had been – they'd even invited him to conga with them, but he'd said, Later, after the cake . . .

At this point, Sabin broke out into loud laughter. Then he began to splutter, laughing and coughing uncontrollably. His fleshy cheeks quivered; I saw past dirty teeth down into his dark maw. He coughed so much he almost choked, but he went on with his story, telling me about the reporter who'd asked, 'So what country are you from?' Traian had only looked even more bewildered – an idiot, what could you say. A Romanian who'd been taken in by fellow Romanians! You could still watch the videos on the internet. Everyone in B. had seen them! For weeks it was all anyone had watched on Internet Hill: *Ţeapă colosală!*

'And after that?'

About six months later, Traian had come knocking at Sabin's door. 'Guv,' he'd said, 'guvnor, have you got work for me?'

He was so skinny and lopsided looking that Sabin hadn't recognised him at first. Even his head was somehow lopsided.

Sabin pulled a face to show me – here, like this.

Things had turned out badly in Spain; Traian was hiding out in his late parents' cottage. He didn't want people to see he was back – not in the state he was in. Maybe Sabin could help him out with a job?

Oh yes, he was quick enough to come begging for help when he needed it. For years it had been 'look at me and my money from Spain' and 'no, no, we'll build the house ourselves'. You'd think, wouldn't you, that he could at least have left Sabin the family ID cards for the elections when he moved away? Like any decent citizen? But no. He had no use for the ID cards in Spain – only needed his passport – but why be decent and help others when it was just as easy not to? He hadn't even given Sabin the ID cards of his late parents! The guy didn't care if he was re-elected or not. Calculating, that's what he was – only out for his own gain.

Traian had defended himself like an idiot. Had he at least donated some of his money to the church in B., Sabin asked. Yes, Traian said, he had. But Sabin only cursed him and called for his dog.

They saw each other once more after that. Sabin had asked Traian to do a small job for him. Nothing too taxing – and anyway, beggars can't be choosers.

When, weeks later, the job still wasn't done, Sabin went round to the old cottage where Traian was living – you couldn't see the place from outside because of the high concrete walls. The yard was overgrown with wild grass and bushes and piled high with junk. You'd have thought no one lived there any more, if it hadn't been for the swanky henhouse – all fixed up with new boards and very spacious. Maybe it was actually meant for geese.

Sabin called out for Traian several times, but there was no reply.

Then he knocked on the door and it yielded and he was hit by a pestilential stench, so strong that he ran straight out again. It was only when he peered through the grimy window that he saw him. Traian was hanging from the wooden ceiling beam, his belly bloated, his protruding tongue bloated too. Dangling there on that string, Sabin thought, he looked like a balloon filled with helium.

Sabin made a dash for it, leaving Traian for others to find.

Then, not long after that, Madame Didina had come to grief and Sabin had heard that she was to be buried in the vault where Count Dracula had his grave. That was when he had the idea!

So he'd known about Dracula's grave all along.

Of course he had. People his age knew their history – not like the young. The amount he'd learnt back then! A staunch national communist he'd been, respected by all his comrades and posted here to keep law and order – to be vigilant.

B. had been the top hunting destination back in the day – for bears, wolves, deer, wild boar, chamois. Comrade Ceaușescu had won 385 super trophies here, all over 400 points and some of them over 700 – world records that had brought great honour to the country. Sabin had got together some fine groups of beaters – and sometimes Comrade Krushchev, Comrade Tito and Comrade Fidel Castro had joined the hunt too. Decent men, they were, knew how to show gratitude to their hosts – Sabin had met them all. B. had been a rich place back then, like all Romania. The young of today had forgotten that. They'd been misled by the West, the capitalist enemy – and by the traitors here at home, the enemies of the working class. Those boyars had been undermining law and order since the beginning of our history – *and* they'd killed the great Prince Vlad Dracula, that was a fact.

Once, Sabin had been in the cemetery at Dracula's grave with the great Comrade Misiuga and some comrade colonels. Comrade Misiuga had plans for a Dracula theme park; he'd applied for permission from on high, but it was taking time and then there was that coup – Sabin wasn't going to call it a revolution – and the moment was past. Then Comrade Agathon was made minister for tourism and the theme-park plans were back on the table. This time, the idea was to build it in Sighişoara or Sibiu, not here in B. The location of Dracula's grave was no longer key to the plan; a grave, they said, could always be replicated.

But there were protests in Bucharest. Students protested against the felling of century-old trees and the damage to the old city centres – and then the priests protested too, concerned that a Dracula theme park would attract foreign Satanists. In the end the project was shelved; the shareholders, Sabin said, laughing gloatingly, never saw their money again.

But he hadn't abandoned his dream of a Dracula theme park in B. This was Vlad Dracula's burial place and Vlad was a legacy of our history – that history that Sabin knew so well. Our Vlad had been the very first national communist. He'd impaled the enemies of the country and the enemies of the working class, the thieves and the social parasites – and he'd kept law and order with a firm fatherly hand. Dracula belonged to the Romanians – why should anyone else cash in on him?

And so Sabin had come up with the bold idea of leaving Traian's supposedly impaled body on Prince Dracula's grave and then pretending to 'discover' whose grave it was.

'But why would you want to impale Traian?' I asked.

Sabin was pleased at my question.

Because everyone here knew what a mess he was. You just had to look at his parents – went around like tramps, the pair of them; his dad even managed to get himself fired from the mill back in Communist times when it was virtually impossible to fire anyone. Not that it changed him – the bloke was incorrigible. Always drinking and thieving and never the slightest respect for the authorities. As for that boy of his – herded the geese barefoot and stole apples. A good-for-nothing, who never made a go of it. The kind that Prince Dracula would have impaled straight out.

In his rotten state he was able to pass as impaled, and Sabin managed to square things with the police and authorities.

One of the Austrians and a party crony helped Sabin place the stinking corpse on Dracula's grave. They did it at night like some kind of laddish prank, but it was also an act of humanity – now no one would ever know that Traian was a suicide; he'd be given a Christian burial.

And at last the work on Dracula Park could begin. The theme park that had already been planned twice over, by two separate ministers for tourism, could now be built – not in Sighișoara or Sibiu, which always got all the perks anyway – but here in B.

And then? What about Traian's wife, Arina?

She'd been hysterical, Sabin said. Screamed around, accused everyone of murdering her husband.

She must have found out about Traian in the papers – seems she'd been working in Bucharest, but she dropped everything and came here. Made all these big accusations about how her husband had been killed – and laid the blame, for whatever reason, on Ata and Sabin.

Then she vanished as if she'd never been back.

'That's it,' Sabin said.

We stood looking at each other in silence.

'Tell me,' he said, 'are we dreaming all this?'

'Even if we were,' I yelled, 'you'd still have to pay for Traian's death.'

XXIV

The Saving Light

I WAS FLOATING ON MY BELLY above B., holding Sabin by his collar. Sabin was clinging to my hand.

'Look down!' I told him. 'Look what you've done!'

At first his eyes had been tightly shut; now that he'd opened them, tears were running down his temples. I don't know if he was crying out of regret or fear, or because the wind in his face was making his eyes water. The long strand of hair that he combed over his bald pate was fluttering free.

He'd stopped moaning; he'd stopped asking me to put him down. He just clung to my hand.

Beneath us lay poor old B. – the ruins, the winding roads, the old weaving mill, the dump in the forest.

'Look down!' I yelled. 'Look!'

'Yes,' he said, 'I'm looking.'

I don't know if he felt regret for his wicked ways or for his impending execution.

He was to die on the same stake as his son; I would watch from the garden table.

But as I sailed over the forest, and day slowly dawned, something happened. Perhaps it was the light dispersing the mist, or the trees beneath us, bursting with light and shade. A bird called. I wondered what kind it was. And Sabin grew heavy in my arms – looking down, I saw that he'd fallen asleep.

A few days later, the journalists were back in B. There were reports of organised crime and of Romanian emigrants with ties to the Sicilian mafia – there was also talk of Dracula and Satanists.

The place was crawling with people; the steep road was lined with corrugated-iron kiosks offering snacks, postcards of neighbouring towns and all kinds of intricately made souvenirs.

I walked through the forest on Yunus's arm, past the old mill to the river. Here too there were people – tourists on the lookout for photo opportunities, for flowers or mushrooms or Dracula.

I saw Sabin sitting by the small pool at the bend in the river. He was surrounded by laughing, shouting women. 'Awesome,' they kept saying. 'This is awesome.'

As we grew nearer, we saw that there was a dog swimming in the pool. It was a black-and-white setter, a hunting dog. Occasionally Sabin would throw a stone into the pool for it and it would swim around, baffled by the sinking stone that it couldn't find to bring back. Everyone laughed at this, and Sabin laughed loudest of all, a slurred, drunken laugh.

There was also a white stick on the river bank, stripped of its bark.

I picked it up and threw it in a high arc to the other side of the river. The dog jumped out of the water and vanished into the undergrowth. Soon afterwards it re-emerged and dropped the stick at my feet; it showed no sign of fearing me.

I don't know how I stopped being a vampire. But I do remember the time I had to comfort Miss Sanda. Geo and I had been brusque with her, accusing her of being a naïve gossip, only interested in prattling about other people's misfortunes (she'd been trying to tell us about Ata's gruesome death). Miss Sanda, who had always had a soft spot for Geo – Ninel, in fact, had always suspected her of being in love with him – stormed out into the garden in a huff. I went and sat next to her under the lilacs and tried to coax her out of her sulk.

All her life, I said, she had thought only of others – always looking out for Mamargot and our family. Maybe it was time she took a look at herself. I told her about the art of the self-portrait – how you looked at yourself in a mirror as you painted yourself, and how the viewers of your painting thought the person you had painted was looking at them, when in fact that person was looking in a mirror. No one thought badly of you for staring in a mirror and thinking about yourself; on the contrary, it made the others, who felt looked at, think about themselves too. That delight in your own gaze was the best way to celebrate life – it was the very art of living.

When I had finished, I fell to childish sobbing. I remember Miss Sanda, bless her, trying to cheer me up: 'Well...'

When we came out from under the shade of the lilacs, we were surprised by the sunset; shimmering red evening light flooded the garden.

And in the pane of the open window, I saw the two of us reflected.

www.sandstonepress.com

Subscribe to our weekly newsletter for events information,
author news, paperback and e-book deals, and the occasional
photo of authors' pets!
bit.ly/SandstonePress

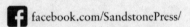 facebook.com/SandstonePress/

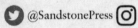 @SandstonePress